FIVE SIX DEADLY MIX

A CASEY FREMONT MYSTERY

FIVE SIX DEADLY MIX

JOHN ACHOR

A CASEY FREMONT MYSTERY

Acacia Imprints

ELKHORN, NEBRASKA

Description: fiction, mystery, female, amateur sleuth

This is a work of fiction. Names, characters, places and incidents are either products of author's imagination or are used fictitiously. Any resemblance to actions or persons, living or dead, events or locales is entirely coincidental: The exception here, is Dr. Jay (Elanka Jayasundera, DNM) who was our vet in real life. Her role in this novel is fictionalized.

Paperback ISBN: 978-1-949601-05-3

Kindle ISBN: 978-1-949601-06-0

Library of Congress Copyright Number: 2018953453

Cataloging in Publication Data on file with Publisher.

ACACIA IMPRINTS

John Achor

Email: john@johnachor.com

Author's Links:

BLOG: http://www.johnachor.wordpress.com/

FACEBOOK: http://www.facebook.com/jachor1

TWITTER: twitter.com/caseyfremont

WEB SITE: www.johnachor.com

3rd Edition, 2018

10 9 8 7 6 5 4 3 2 1

READER REVIEWS ABOUT
FIVE, SIX – DEADLY MIX

Another fast-moving story that made me feel like I was riding in those fast cars, sitting around the table eating goodies, fitting bits of information together to catch the murderer. And on top of that I was just a little enthralled with that good looking detective and the mysterious investigator dressed all in black. This is the third book in the Casey Fremont series and I have read them all. This is a good read for all mystery readers.

GLYNDA

As a longtime fan of John Achor (as well as personal friend), I have read all of John's Casey Fremont novels and marvel at how he has kept her actions challenging and the cast of characters who surround her interesting and expanding. As a resident of Arkansas and living near Little Rock, I can vouch for the accuracy of John's geographical references. Another good job John, can't wait for the next one.

MARJORIE M.

OTHER BOOKS BY JOHN ACHOR

Casey Fremont mysteries
One, Two – Kill A Few
Three, Four – Kill Some More
Five, Six – Deadly Mix

Alex Hilliard thrillers
Assault on the Presidency

DEDICATION

To Lexus and Dr. Jay

ACKNOWLEDGMENTS

My profound thanks go to my family who always give me inspiration and encouragement. Thanks to any number of places like coffeehouses or bagel shops where an author can write. Also, to casinos which provide many places where an author can relax while his wife beats up their slot machines.

My thanks also go to a Hot Springs critique group: Chenyn Allen, DeAnn Almond, Dick Cecil, Gene Forsyth, Carol Fox, Nancy Smith Gibson, Chap Harper, Adam Harvey, Carole Katchen, Bill Shuler, and Sherri Ungerer. (I feel I've missed someone and for that I apologize). This group shared their time, knowledge and expertise providing me with more assistance than an author could expect. If there are any errors in this work, they are mine. If I strayed from the straight and narrow, it was due to writer's license or fictionalization and not pure error.

More about our vet, Dr. Jay, later, but her name bears repeating here. Her knowledge was invaluable when I was writing about the last days of Casey's cat, PK (Psycho Kitty). Her compassion was like a rock to cling to when the end came for both our felines, Lexus and Betsy. Thank you, Dr. Jay.

FOREWORD

SPOILER ALERT – this section reveals some plot points

I know animal lovers out there (especially our oldest daughter) are likely to be upset, or even angry with me, for the plot twist I took allowing PK (Casey's cat, Psycho Kitty) to die. I wasn't too happy myself, but I felt I needed to do it. Lurking deep in me was the thought of losing our oldest cat, Lexus, soon. Lexie was becoming frailer by the week. She wasn't ill as I was writing this, but she's eighteen years old, her sight is gone, her hearing is going and she has a bit of arthritis in her right front leg. Her back legs are great, and she can still launch herself up on couches, beds, and window seats with little effort. It's the getting down that's a problem. I purchased a set of animal steps so she could get down from our bed where she still spends most nights.

With that in mind, I think that PK became a natural part of the plot, and a way for me to steel myself for Lexie's passing. You can see a picture of Lexus (and her obituary) on my web site: johnachor.com on the About Me > Author Bio menu selection.

In the story, Dr. Jay (Elanka Jayasundera, DVM our real-life vet) gives Casey three pieces of paper regarding the loss of a pet. They are mentioned by title in the story, and I have included them at the end of this book in the Appendix.

One more piece of business before we get started. Some time ago, I sponsored a contest: "help me name this book" with the winner becoming a character in this novel. Two ladies provided the answer. One suggested *Deadly* and the other submitted *Mix*. I combined the two answers and Karen Jordan and Janet Liszka became: Janet Jordan. Thanks to Janet and Karen for your patience and your help coming up with: *Five, Six – Deadly Mix*.

1

MY NAME IS CASEY FREMONT, AND I'VE BEEN MAKING a decent living working temporary jobs since my husband dumped me. I may get the last laugh yet. Bambi, his girlfriend, left him. Now he has become the dumpee.

Today I'm heading for an initial interview to prepare for my latest temp job. The last two didn't work out that well; both put me in the middle of multiple murders and mayhem. I vowed this position would be different—no troubles, no dead guys, just a good paycheck for a while. Well, a gal can hope, can't she?

I'm in this current mess because my on-again off-again boyfriend, Dennis Epstein, asked me to "join him." I thought he was asking me out on a date, but he told me I could do him a big favor by acting as a Confidential Informant. Only he referred to it as being a CI—as those in the law enforcement call it. I was up for the adventure, but disappointed that our relationship was being put on hold. Did I mention Dennis is a detective sergeant with the Little Rock Police Department?

Federal agencies suspect Medicare fraud at Little Rock General Hospital. In addition, there have been a couple of strange deaths of hospital personnel. Nothing provable but nonetheless, unexplained. To worm my way in, I went through Rutledge Trublood, a semi-likable letch who owns the TrueTemp Employment Agency. He made all the contacts so I didn't have to show up cold and arouse suspicions. I also like this company because a good friend and confidant, Rebecca Rider, works there as his receptionist. Becca assisted me solving cases I've stumbled into.

The Feds are involved because of the Medicare fraud, and Special Agent Montgomery Williams of the FBI asked Dennis to join the investigation since the deaths at the hospital could be related to the suspected fraud. Dennis invited me along because he knows me: I'm a damn good investigator and persistent as hell.

2

BEFORE I SHOW UP AT THE HOSPITAL, THE FBI SPECIAL
Agent assigned to the case wanted to meet with me, and according to Dennis, he "needed to assess my capabilities." Big whoop.
Tomorrow I am scheduled to report to the hospital for a specific
job assignment. I wondered what the FBI agent planned to do
if I didn't pass muster.

Dennis and I met him at a restaurant out where the buses
don't run; far enough from the hospital to avoid being recognized. I looked around as we entered, and headed for a booth
on the right and so far back it was barely inside the building.

Dennis said, "Casey, this is FBI Special Agent Montgomery
Williams. Montgomery, meet Casey Fremont."

With the formalities behind us, Williams took over the conversation. Following a couple of perfunctory comments, he said,
"Of course, Casey, I will be your handler and we will meet at
least three times per week, and—"

"Whoa, Hoss," I said. "Do you have any idea why I made a
beeline to this table?"

"Well, I assumed Dennis described me..."

He wore a haircut from back in the day—clippers all around,
white sidewall style. The close-cut hair was topped with a cropped
flattop. I wondered if he thought he was fooling anyone; his forehead must have been two inches lower when he first adopted
that style. I shook my head. "I recognized you as soon as I came
in here." He started to say something, so I held my hand up,
palm toward him. "As soon as I stepped inside this place, your
appearance screamed Feeb—FED, and I don't need to be meeting

with anyone who can jeopardize my cover that quick. Is this the first time they put you on an undercover operation without adult supervision?"

Dennis was sitting next to the agent. I shifted my gaze to him and was pleased to see the hint of a smile. "Who would you like to meet with, Casey?" he said. "I could do it."

"Oh, Dennis, you're nearly as bad. I want Becca to be my intermediary." I turned to the agent and said, "She's with the TrueTemp Employment Agency—and she can report to one or both of you."

I saw a frown on the Feeb's face. Dennis put a hand on top of mine and said, "Becca has been a great help to Casey. In the past, she's been instrumental in helping solve a couple of cases."

"Ms. Fremont, what got you involved in solving crimes?" the agent said.

"At first it was just something to do and keep my mind occupied. I needed the extra activity to wiggle out of the blue funk my ex-husband left me in."

Williams stared at me for a minute before frowning. He said, "Bad marriage, eh?"

I gave him an eye roll and thought *this guy has all the deductive reasoning of a squid.* I started to respond, thought better of it and concentrated on my coffee cup.

Dennis came riding to the rescue, and his attempt at conversation fell flat.

Williams didn't seem in the mood for further discussion. He confirmed a couple of points with Dennis and excused himself. Dennis slipped back into the booth opposite me.

When Williams was out the door, Dennis said, "Wow, Casey; I don't think you made any friends with your comments."

"Did I say anything that was untrue?"

"No, but damn, Casey, you didn't have to verbally body slam him. I barely recognize you—sort of out of character. When I first met you, you didn't have the temperament to do that."

I said, "Then I guess I've come a long way in the self-esteem department."

"Yes, you have," Dennis said. "You told Agent Williams you needed to get out of a blue funk. How are you doing?"

"At first, all this sleuthing was just a diversion for my mind. But the more I do, the more I enjoy being able to lead a group—even if we are amateurs—and hold my own against the bad guys. I've proved a great deal to myself."

"I'm proud of you for leaving your ex in the dust and getting on with your life."

I gave Dennis my best smile. "I've got to get out of here. It's getting late and I need to set up some ground rules with Becca."

"Before you go, there's something else you should know. You may have a deadline to get the goods on this bunch," he said.

Dennis went on to explain his sources on the street told him the fraud and thefts may be coming to an end. "I don't have anything firm on a date, but the best estimate I can make is mid-June, so let's use June fifteenth as our deadline."

"If the scams are working, why would the perps call it quits?"

"The word is, they want to stash several million for the main players, close down the operation and emigrate to a country without extradition treaties with the United States."

"They'll need passports. Can't Homeland Security or the FBI trace them in short order?"

Dennis let out a long sigh. "Even with all the tight security, it's not hard to come up with a fake ID. If they apply for the passports using an alias, there's no way to track them. My informants haven't been able to give me any leads on the fake names."

"Well, June fifteenth is two and a half months away. That should give us ample time to wrap this up," I said.

"Let's hope so."

I gathered my belongings and headed for the TrueTemp Agency to catch Becca before she left for the day.

3

NOTHING MUCH EVER CHANGES AT THE TRUETEMP Agency where, Becca Rider is still the receptionist. Rutledge Trublood, the owner, is still a letch. Becca continues to make him get his own coffee and seldom shares her donuts with him.

When I first met Becca, she was a size twenty-two and out of shape. She exercised and dieted until was down to an eighteen, which ain't bad for a black gal her size. The other change she made was to reward herself with a new car. Not new, but a model she always wanted: a Firebird T-top in British racing green. She also treated herself to a course in high-speed driving in Phoenix.

We adjourned to the break room. I ran the particulars of my CI stint, and said, "You up for another escapade?"

"Will we get a chance to follow someone again? I never had so much fun as when we were chasing Romeo."

I recalled the chase. Becca showed off her training from the Bondurant high-speed driving school. "I'm glad you were having fun, 'cause I closed my eyes for most of it." Next I recounted my conversation with the FBI and Dennis.

"Damn, girl. You never used to have the nerve to lay it on like that. How'd he take it?"

"I don't suppose he was real happy about what I said. He didn't hang around too long—but darn it, I was right. A blind man could ID him as a Fed from a mile away—in the pitch black."

"Ain't you exaggerating a bit?"

I described him in detail: shoes, suit, tie, and haircut. "What would you deduce about him?"

"Feeb," she said with a grin on her face.

We laid out a plan of attack. As soon as I got my assignment at Little Rock General, I would contact her. I wanted both of us to get the lay of the land—to be able to navigate the building.

Experience told me hospitals can be confusing. New construction added to the original building; wings and el's attached, floors that didn't match up from one section to the next.

We established ground rules: how and when we would contact one another, rendezvous points—we would add more once we understood the building's layout—we also arranged duress and warning words to alert the other to danger.

"Is Rutledge behaving himself?" I said.

"As far as I know he is. And I don't cut him much slack."

"No recent groping?"

Becca laughed out loud. "I think the time you put the crotch squeeze on his privates cured him."

Becca looked up at the clock over the snack room sink. "Ol' Rutledge is gone by now. Gotta lock up the place."

I followed her out of the office and waited as she secured the door. Down in the elevator, a brief nod from each of us as we parted in the parking lot. "You stay safe, girl," Becca said as she walked away.

The weather was moderate and I could enjoy a breeze whipping into my convertible. On the way home I put the top down on my Mustang and considered Becca's parting words. I couldn't imagine those perpetrating medical fraud would be dangerous. But, then—long ago I received an axiom: hope for the best, prepare for the worst. Better to be prepared and not caught flat-footed.

* * *

I'm sure my roomies Effie Tremayne and Aaron Kincaid will be disappointed. They got used to being amateur sleuths and played a big role in solving the last two crimes. Over dinner I told Effie and Aaron what I was up to and how Dennis Epstein involved me in his business. The phone rang, and it was Dennis. I said, "Your ears must be burning. I was just talking about you."

"Casey, since you are now a registered CI, I won't be able to see you…socially, that is."

"Well, there hasn't been much of that going on around here. I've almost forgotten what you look like. Give me a hint. Are you the black gay guy living at my condo? Nah…I guess not, that's Aaron…" I left the comment floating in the air hoping to lay a guilt trip on Dennis.

"I'm sorry about that," Dennis said. "When this is over, I hope we can remedy the situation."

Pleasantries out of the way, we both said goodnight.

I also briefed the two of them on the possible deadline of June fifteenth. Aaron rose and said, "I need to hit the books and then bed. Big exam on Design and Planning Theories in the morning." During the past six months, he used his time between flights to further his education. His job as a flight attendant for a local airline allowed him breaks during which he could pursue his studies as an architect. We pitched in and arranged his part of my condo with a drafting table along with all the necessary supplies—a bit crowded, but livable.

I also helped Effie buy and set up a sewing machine, mannequin, and a pattern table in her room. During the time we've been sharing the condo, she developed her interest in clothing into a burgeoning, albeit part time, vocation.

Wow, I thought. When she arrived from a small town in Arkansas and came to live with me, she had little or no clothing sense. Now she was designing and selling women's fashions. Effie was earning a decent income from the casual business-wear she put together. Her main thrust was to create pieces in complimentary colors that could be mixed and matched, creating the appearance of a large wardrobe with modest investment.

Big day ahead and I had the jitters. I felt this was at the beginning of what could be a difficult time. I did my best to project the image of my place at the hospital, but that effort failed. I snuggled into the covers for what I expected to be less than a good night's sleep.

4

THE NIGHT WAS NOT AS RESTLESS AS I EXPECTED. With a reasonable night's sleep and one of Effie's breakfasts behind me, I was ready to sally forth to slay dragons.

I was edgy as I pulled into the employee parking area of the Little Rock General Hospital. In the past, the bad guys came after me; this time I was going after them…on purpose. I found myself hoping the dragons would be small ones.

An empty Visitor slot near the main doors beckoned me. The weatherman on the morning show forecasted rain so I put the top up before I got out and locked the door. Inside, the building emitted the aura of a hospital—cold temperature, the aroma of cleaning fluids and freshly polished marble flooring. A volunteer staffing the reception desk directed me to the Human Resources office.

At my destination, the nameplate on her desk read: Mrs. Harriet Manfriedy. I learned from the receptionist she was the Chief of Human Resources for the entire hospital for matters of personnel, and sure enough the title leapt from her nameplate. She glanced at her watch. "Right on time, Ms. Fremont. I like punctuality."

"Please call me Casey."

She stood, reached across her desk to take my hand. As she released it, she gestured toward a pair of chairs facing her desk. She was wearing a potent fragrance I didn't recognize. I'll never understand why some women wear that much perfume, especially in a hospital setting.

A file on her desk was adjusted square with the front edge. She flipped open the folder, and then moved it so it was again aligned parallel with her desk front and exactly in the middle.

Anal retentive I bet if I used a tape measure, the distance from each side of the folder to the edges of the desk wouldn't vary a quarter of an inch. She picked up the left most pencil from a covey of five, lying side by side, sharpened to the same length and again aligned with the edge of the desk. She tapped the erasure end on the top page of what I assumed was a sheaf of papers about me.

"I see from the information sent over from the TrueTemp Agency, you've a wealth of experience," she said. "You last worked for a legal firm and before that a computer technology company. Where did you get the background for those positions?"

I didn't want to go deep into my history even though the answer was simple. Eight years married to a dipstick who said and repeated, "No wife of mine is going to continue working." With so much time on my hands, I took courses and classes on a wide variety of subjects: law, gun marksmanship and ownership, Tai Chi, Taekwondo, yoga, karate, plus I wedged in several computer science courses and even one about jumping out of airplanes.

"A lot of time on my hands, so I took classes," I said hoping this explanation would suffice. It did and her attention returned to my file.

Mrs. Manfriedy handed me a clipboard with several sheets attached. She explained the need for each form and added, "I've indicated with sticky arrows the places where you must sign and date each one."

Of course, you have, I thought. I wondered how she would react if I asked to use one of her precisely aligned pencils. I didn't. I pulled a pen and notepad from my purse. I learned long ago it is simpler to bring background data written down rather than depend on my memory.

When I handed the clipboard back, she made a couple of phone calls. "They're shorthanded in the pharmacy area. Don't tell me you're also a licensed pharmacist." I shook my head. Inside

I smiled because I do have a license but it's a concealed-carry permit for a weapon, not to dispense meds.

"Don't worry about it. You should be well qualified to handle the paperwork over there. I've asked one of their techs to come and escort you back. On the way, we'll get you an ID badge so you can move around on your own." She stood and said, "It's a pleasure to have you with us, Ms. Fremont. We will be conducting a background check on you as well. The chief of pharmacy told me I could send you over and we'd get the results later."

Nothing like being wanted.

Her assistant appeared as if by magic and led me from the office. Outside I started for the exit, but the middle age woman said, "Not so fast. We have more for you before you can go to work. You need an ID badge and I can take care of that here."

"Okay, is that all?"

"Hardly, you will need a drug test and a tuberculosis test as well."

"I had a TB test last fall. Is it necessary to repeat it?"

The assistant put a stern look on her face. "We don't take anyone's word on this. They seem to be in a hurry to put you to work. We won't wait for the outcome of the tests, but we still have to do them." Mrs. Manfriedy's assistant made a phone call, and in a few minutes a nurse arrived.

The RN extracted a small instrument from a sterile package and injected something under the skin on my left arm. She said, "Normally we have to wait for the results of the test, but I guess someone wants you to get to work right away. Please stop by this office for the next two days so I can check the test results."

Mrs. Manfriedy's assistant handed me a small paper cup. "Let's not forget a specimen for the drug test." She pointed toward the restroom. I returned, being careful not to spill the contents of the cup.

Next, a brief stop in the section just outside Mrs. Manfriedy's office. Fast, efficient. I clipped the new picture badge to my jacket.

The assistant said, "Mrs. Manfriedy told me we can skip the new employee orientation. If you're still here next week, I'll schedule a time for you."

Another greasy skid, I thought, hoping all the attention I was getting wouldn't blow my cover.

A lady in dark blue scrubs entered the cubicle and said, "If you're Casey Fremont, I'm here to collect you. My name's Janet Jordan."

We shook hands and she set off at a brisk pace. I lagged behind, doing my best to mentally catalog the route to the pharmacy area. The Yellow Brick Road music from The Wizard of Oz was going through my head as we rounded corner after corner. I pushed that out of my head, remembering the serious business of spying on the employees was about to begin.

5

ON THE WAY, JANET BRIEFED ME ON MY DUTIES IN the pharmacy. I would be matching paperwork to patients, making sure the names corresponded and label coding was correct. A reasonably simple task—confirm the right patient was charged and keep the insurance companies happy.

When we arrived in the pharmacy, I waited near the door where I could see the boss' desk. This area was like any office space; the actual dispensing pharmacy was off to the side behind two doors, which I assumed were locked. Janet spoke to the department head, Molly Rasmussen, and asked her if she would like to interview me.

The paper flow was from individual pharmacists to this administrative section. Molly shook her head and said, "No, put her to work."

According to Janet, Molly took charge of incoming paperwork and separated it into four stacks. She doled out three of the piles to Janet, me, and a third administrative person who was not at work when Janet and I arrived.

The fourth stack Molly reserved for herself and they resided in the top left drawer of her desk. She referred to it as her Inbox, and it was off-limits to us mere mortals. She said, "Habit I guess," and she picked up the unclaimed pile and added it to her own.

Strange lady, I thought. But then, the world is full of eccentrics; why not the hospital as well?

Janet explained the process to me; it was close to a no-brainer like walking and chewing gum. I watched Molly and Janet as I shuffled the paperwork from my In pile to the Outbox. Molly seemed a dour woman, with a look on her face that reminded me of a person with a sour stomach. I started to reach for the roll of antacid tablets in my purse but thought better of it. Even her hair matched her personality—pulled back in a severe bun at the back of her head. I also pondered the secretive way she guarded her *personal* stack of paperwork. She emphasized the "off-limits" aspect of that drawer when describing her desk. The one time she got up to head down the hall, she locked her desk. A bit excessive, I thought.

Janet was an opposite. Her fresh scrubbed appearance matched the flowers in a small vase on her desk. My hunch was she changed them every morning. She wore her hair short with a tight curl all over. The other thing separating her from our boss was the constant smile on her face. She would no doubt be a good person to provide information about the hospital.

My assumption was correct. She showed me the way to the cafeteria for our lunch break, and she enjoyed talking. It was easy to lead her into most any subject I wanted. Earlier I saw her as bright and fresh and guessed she had all the male attention she wanted. And maybe a bit more than she desired. She was eager to relate details to a new listener. I pressed her for specifics about the hospital in general and the pharmacy in particular. She told me there were rumors on the hospital grapevine the two recent deaths were more than the suicides they were reported to be.

"What do you mean? What could have happened to the two people who died?" I said.

"They weren't the suicide type. Matter of fact, I knew one of the ladies who died personally."

The look on her face as she scanned the room said: I've opened my big mouth again. I said, "How so?"

She leaned across the table and lowered her voice. "The word around here is someone was upset…no, was mad at them."

I pulled a bit more from her—one of the dead women worked in the office Janet and I were in. She was the one I didn't meet;

no wonder—she's dead. The other casualty worked in accounting as a liaison between billing and collections sections.

Janet said, "We better get back to work. Molly can be hell on wheels when she thinks I've taken too long a break."

I was sorry we didn't have more time because she was a fount of information. At the same time, I didn't want to get her in hot water with her boss. I settled on a lunch date with Janet for the next day.

Around two, Molly sent me on a cafeteria run. She likes an afternoon ice cream snack. I planned on picking up a cup of coffee for myself and asked Janet what she wanted.

"Thanks, but I don't need anything," Janet said. She turned her back to Molly and whispered. "She doesn't like the rest of us to have treats in here."

I shrugged, turned and left the office. The cafeteria was a ten minute walk. Fortunately, decent signage appeared at each corridor. At every turn I saw the word "Cafeteria" and an arrow pointing the way. I stepped through the door and did a double take. Falcon was sitting in a far corner with a large coffee cup in front of him.

He saw me as soon as I entered and gave me a barely perceptible head shake. I understood; he didn't want company. I met Falcon when I temped at a law firm. He worked for the private investigation company hired by the lawyers. Falcon always wore black or subdued color clothing so he could blend into the background. He played a major role in the capture of a killer we dubbed Romeo. We also dated a couple of times. I watched him pull a pen from his pocket and scribble something on his napkin.

I paid for my coffee and an ice cream bar for Molly. She either forgot to give me money or she makes a habit out of lapses of memory. On my way out, I could see Falcon's chair was empty— he slipped out without my noticing him. The napkin was still on the table he vacated. I pretended to have trouble balancing my load. I put the ice cream down and shifted my coffee to the other hand. It was simple to palm the note as I retrieved Molly's snack.

His message was succinct. "Undercover—I'll find you in the parking lot—your car at 5:30." I put the crumpled note into the pocket of my slacks. No sense leaving clues for others to find. The rest of the day was slow as slogging through quicksand.

Apparently, Janet changed her mind and we took a late afternoon break together. I picked a seat at a table in the cafeteria and this time she grabbed the chair next to me rather than the one across the table. She tore a spare napkin in half, then in half again. Working off nervous energy, I guess. She leaned close and her voice was a bare whisper.

"I've been thinking about our discussion earlier," Janet said. "I've been thinking about Gloria and Roberta…"

The look on my face must have been a clue.

She said, "Oh, didn't you know the names of the dead ladies?"

"Nope…but go ahead with your thought."

"Well, their names were Gloria Sexton and Roberta Blackwood. Three days before each death, a rumor spread around the hospital that they were in trouble."

"What sort of trouble?"

Janet paused before she answered. "Don't know. I figured it was something about job performance. Like they might get fired."

I didn't push her further. We finished our snacks and went back to the office.

6

FIVE-THIRTY ARRIVED BEFORE I WENT NUTS WAITING. I stashed my work in a neat pile ready for tomorrow, said goodnight to Janet and Molly, and left the office.

Steam rose from the asphalt in the parking lot. Remnants of the rain the morning weatherman forecasted. I had to do a double-look around to be sure I remembered where I parked the Mustang. Arriving at my destination, my car was nowhere in sight. I did a slow three-sixty turn and still wasn't sure where I was going. First panic thought; someone stole my car.

I pulled the keys from my purse and pressed the alarm button on the remote. A horn honked two rows back and right of my position. In less than a minute I was at the driver's door and silenced the honking alarm. As I reached for the door handle, a voice behind me said, "Good job, Casey. Now everyone knows where we are." I recognized Falcon's voice. He continued, "Get the doors open so we can get in. Don't want anyone to know I'm here with you."

I punched the Unlock button on the remote and Falcon was in the car before I could move. I said, "What's the big cloak-and-dagger routine?"

"There're some bad dudes around this place. They've already killed two women and I don't think it'll stop at two."

I said, "You sure those women didn't commit suicide?

"I'm certain. There's a bunch of money in play. Well worth the effort. That's why I was asked to look around."

I quizzed him on who his employer was and he ignored the question. Rather than answer, he asked me what I was doing at the hospital. I debated the question in my mind, weighing the warnings Dennis gave me against the valuable help Falcon might be to me. Falcon won. "Okay," I said, "can you tell me what you're looking for?"

"Sure. We believe a group of individuals are stealing drugs from the hospital. Worth a fortune out on the street—illicit drugs and bad people are a dangerous combination." After a pause he said, "And what brings you to this den of iniquity?"

"The FBI came to the local police and asked for help. The Feds are sure there is rampant Medicare fraud at the hospital."

Falcon was silent for several minutes. The wait was becoming unbearable, and he spoke at last. "I'm wondering if these two cases could be connected…possible, but I doubt it. Seems like we have two groups involved in activities that make them dangerous to anyone snooping around in their business."

"Who are you watching? I may be able to locate some info that might help you. And, I'd like to know who to stay away from."

Falcon said, "I appreciate the offer to help. I haven't been on the case long enough to form opinions or identify the perps. Give me a day or two and I'll get back to you on that. Have you uncovered anything on your end?"

"I've run into some strange activities and people, but little to go on as far as the fraud goes." I jingled my keys and slid one into the ignition lock. "How did you know I was here?"

"I've been watching you for several days. Casey, you need to keep better track of everything going on all around you."

Ever the stern disciplinarian, Falcon went silent. I said, "I'd like you a lot more if you'd have a positive word to say every once and a while."

"Sorry. I've stayed alive for a long time by being cautious. I'd hate to see anything bad happen to you." He flipped the passenger door open and left my car.

I guess that's the closest to a touch of concern I'll get from him, I thought. He's right; I can't afford to slip up or let someone slip up on me. I'll keep an eye over my shoulder from now on.

7

THAT NIGHT AT HOME I TALKED TO MY ROOMIES about my day. I told them I ran into Falcon. Both Aaron and Effie knew him from our previous *crime-fighting* escapades.

Effie prodded me for details about my work and asked what Falcon was investigating. I said, "I don't think Falcon would want me discussing his activities without telling him first."

Effie nodded. "Then, how about your day? What did you do? Did you find any of the fraud cases?"

Aaron returned to the kitchen table and I covered my day—the details of my workload and described the people I'd met. I categorized the people: Mrs. Manfriedy was the most likely to have OCD. Molly Rasmussen, my immediate boss, was too secretive; I figured her for a possible participant in the Medicare fraud. Janet, a co-worker, was friendly enough and I thought I could get more information from her about the hospital and the people who worked there. "So far I think I've only met the small fish. I need to find out who they work for and who is running the fraud. And, I suppose I also need to discover how and what they're doing."

Just then, Psycho Kitty, came racing into the living room heading for the large trompe l'oeil mural. Instead of his usual leap, splat, slide, he pulled up short and sat looking at the table in the mural. We all exchanged glances and Effie said, "Is there something wrong with PK? Seems he's been acting strange of late."

Aaron shook his head. "He's been acting sluggish lately." Then he made one of those "come here" noises to PK and the cat started toward him.

At the last minute, PK veered away from Aaron and headed toward me. He stopped just short of the chair and sat there measuring the distance up to my lap. I am still amazed that cats can judge the distance to jump, and then expend the absolute minimum energy to their rear legs to land on the desired spot. That's exactly what PK did, and the next second he was on my lap. He did a two-turn circle and settled down with his chin on my leg.

Effie said, "How old is PK?"

"I don't really know what year he was born," I said, "but he's fourteen or fifteen and he's become a huge part of my life." I was stroking his soft coat and looked at PK for a several moments. Then I turned to Effie and Aaron, and said, "I guess I need to take him to see the vet. I wish I wasn't so busy at work right now. Being short one person in the office, the Medicare paperwork is piling up. I barely have any time to snoop around."

"I'm off tomorrow. I could take him in," Aaron said.

"Thank you, Aaron," I said, "For now I can concentrate on how I can recruit Janet as my own CI."

Aaron said, "I won't be able to hang around for any tests Dr. Jay may run. I'll be leaving early tomorrow evening and won't be back till late Sunday."

That still leaves me with a pair of problems—Janet and PK. Recruiting Janet shouldn't be difficult; she seems to have an adventurous bent. "I'll be able to pick up PK," I said to Aaron. *I wonder why I'm feeling nervous about PK's condition.*

8

I SPENT THE NEXT DAY TALKING TO JANET AS OFTEN as I could find the time. I needed to figure out what her motivations are; maybe that will make it easier to get her to help me. I worked on it all morning and over lunch with little progress. When we took an afternoon break and settled at a table, she took a long breath and leaned back in her chair. I could tell something was in the air and wondered if I should remain silent or if a probing question might work better.

I kept quiet, and so did she. I was about to stand up and scream when Janet leaned forward and spoke. "Casey, can I trust you?"

I nodded and said, "Of course you can. Anything or everything is safe with me."

"I'm worried." She stopped and glanced around the room.

The look on her face mirrored the *worry* she expressed. "Go ahead, Janet. What are you worried about?"

She looked around the room again and lowered her voice to a whisper. "Two women have died—supposed to be suicides. But I don't believe it. And one of them was from the section where we work. I'm not sure what's going on, but that one hit too close to home. I'm wondering if I'm in danger as well."

"Why do you think you might be in danger? Are you doing anything wrong?" She shook her head. "Are you aware of any hanky-panky at the hospital?"

Again, she shook her head. Now it was my turn to look around to see if anyone could overhear our conversation. The coast seemed clear; I leaned back and pondered what I was about to do. Enough, Casey—make a decision and get with it.

With my mind made up, I leaned forward. "Janet, now it's my turn to ask if I can trust you." All I got was head movement, but this time she nodded. "If what I am about to tell you gets out, I may be the next fatality." I waited for the words to sink in.

She nodded her head again and whispered, "You can trust me."

I was about to violate every rule in the book about working undercover. "Janet, I'm here at the behest of the local police and the FBI." Her eyes widened and dilated. "Actually, I'm a covert Confidential Informant. As a CI, I don't have any real authority; I just snoop around and gather any evidence I can find."

"You mean that I won't get a secret decoder ring?"

I loved her sense of humor already and my sincere desire was not to get her killed. "You're right. No decoder rings, no authority, and we have to look out for ourselves. There are some folks who can lend us a hand, but they won't be nearby."

"Who?"

"That's not important right now." I didn't want to reveal all my cards; after all I could be making a gross error in judgment going *this* far.

"Well then, what are we looking for?" she said

I gave her a general run down on my mission and told her to keep an eye on Molly. "I would love to find out what she hides in that locked desk drawer."

"I bet I can help with that." She waited to be sure she had my full attention. "One day she had to go home sick and gave me the key to her desk. She never asked me to return it; I think she forgot all about it."

"Janet, you just made my day."

9

IT WAS NEARLY TIME TO SHUT DOWN THE OFFICE and head for home. Molly locked her desk and started for the door saying, "I've got to get to an appointment and I'm running late."

Janet and I gave her enough time to clear the building before we began whispering our plans to each other. I said, "The first thing I want is to get a look at that top left drawer. The one she seems to guard with an undue zeal. After all, it's only work, isn't it?"

"Okay, here's the key to Molly's desk," Janet said. "I'm going to look around the office for a larger stash of her secret papers."

"Why do you call them secret?"

"What else would you call routine paperwork she doesn't want anyone to look at?"

While Janet went exploring, I unlocked the infamous top left drawer of Molly's desk. I riffled through the stack of papers and saw nothing untoward. I checked all four edges of the papers looking for some kind of snare she used to protect her hoard. And I found it. There was a piece of thread taped to the bottom of the drawer; she tucked the loose end between two work folders. If, when she returned, the strand was not in the same place she left it; she could be certain someone was snooping around. She was being far too paranoid and careful about work papers to be on the up and up. The skin on the back of my neck tingled. I raised my head and glanced around the office half expecting to find Molly staring at me. She wasn't.

I lifted the folder on top of the thread and noted the name on the file just below it. I needed to make sure I kept them in their original order, otherwise Molly might become suspicious. Then I lifted the files out in two stacks and placed them on the desktop. I used my phone to snap several shots of the stacks of file folders as I moved them.

I didn't see any obvious clues in the paperwork. Looking at the type of reimbursement, I did notice several claims that fell into a group that was easy to "upgrade" to receive a higher payout. I was not able to quantify a problem, so fanned the folders showing the information tab. That would give me a claimant's name and the type of illness. Using the photos on my phone, I was able to replace the folders and the thread back into Molly's drawer in the exact order and position as when I opened it.

Janet returned and I asked her what she'd found. I took a shrug and a head shake a sign she came up empty. We agreed to head for home. I told her I planned to arrive early enough to beat Molly to work. "I want to see if she has any clue that someone was looking around."

10

I SLEPT WELL OVER THE WEEKEND, EXCEPT FOR A couple of dreams where Molly's henchmen caught me and were about to inflict severe pain upon my body. Friday night I found a note from Aaron telling me he was leaving on a two-day trip. The note said he had news for me and would talk to me after the weekend.

Monday morning, I was out the door before Effie or Aaron were even up, and I forgot about Aaron's note. I grabbed a quick bite at a fast-food drive-through on the way to the hospital. When I entered our workspace, I was the only warm body in sight. I pulled out the pile of work I put away Friday night and busied myself with looking like I was really working. My mind wasn't in it but I kept my head down. I also kept sneaking peeks toward Molly's desk.

Molly breezed into the office and looked at me. "That's what I like to see, employees on time and busy at work."

I paid attention to her movements, hoping I could pick up on any reactions she might display. She sat down and pulled a key ring from her purse and used one of them to unlock that infamous upper right desk storage space. Molly leaned over the drawer and with intent concentration scanned the open drawer. I could tell there was more attentiveness than needed to unload the files to her desktop. It looked to me like she was doing a mental double take. She cocked her head and held the pose for several seconds. I held my breath waiting for her to look at me and show some kind of threatening gesture.

Molly leaned back and appeared to be reaching for the work folders. I gave a sigh of relief and stood up heading for the water cooler. My path would take me close to her desk.

As I passed, I could see her use extreme care to lift the stack of files and check to see where the string rested. When she saw the file below the string, there was a almost imperceptible smile on her face. I wondered what the expression would have been if I didn't discover her trap. I imagine her demeanor would have been harsh.

Janet arrived a few minutes later and I did my best not to look at her. When I did sneak a quick peek, she seemed to be going through a similar exercise. On my way back to my workstation, I stopped at her desk and whispered about meeting during our morning break. She nodded.

I was getting antsy and the time crawled. Nine forty-five was as long as I could stretch my wait. "I think I'll take an early break," I said in a stage voice. "Janet, are you up for a break now?"

Without answering, Janet stood and headed for the door. I followed tingling with excitement. We turned a corner in the hall and I couldn't wait any longer. "You didn't say much Friday night—did you find anything while you were prowling around Friday?"

"I think I know where those *secret* files go when Molly is finished with them," I said.

"Well, are you going to share?"

11

JANET WINKED AT ME AND SAID, "LATER WHEN WE get to the cafeteria."

I was beginning to think Janet already figured me out and knew what it took to drive me up a wall. I smiled and shrugged my shoulders.

Janet took the hallway straight ahead rather than the right turn toward the cafeteria. "How come we're going this way?"

"Keep up and I'll show you. I have a surprise for you," Janet said.

After a few minutes, she rounded a familiar corner and I realized we were near the Human Resources department. I picked up my pace so Janet wouldn't leave me behind. "So, you think it's someone in HR?"

"Not just *in* HR, but the head of it."

"What makes you think Manfriedy is part of this fraud?"

"Well, who has almost unfettered access to all parts of the hospital? And, who is far enough up the food chain to get away with what she's doing? And, finally, I saw a batch of file folders on her desk."

"You think a bunch of file folders means she's a crook?"

"Not just random folders. I remember seeing this bunch in our office and they were some of the ones that came from Molly's desk drawer."

I said, "Can we get to them so I can use my phone to take pictures of these folders?"

Janet nodded and pressed on toward area occupied by HR. Even from the entryway I could tell that Mrs. Manfriedy was not in her office. Janet pointed out the stack of folders in question and I whispered to her and told her to create a distraction. "I'll get the pictures then."

She moved to a corner of the area and began talking in a loud enough voice that no one in the office could do anything but look at her. I smiled at her and eased into the department head's office. I gave the stack a nudge so the folders fanned out a bit. When most of the folder tabs were visible, I brought up my phone and snapped two pictures. I moved the folders back into their original position and stepped out of Manfriedy's office.

As I left the area, Janet said, "And, that's all I've got to say on that subject." She stopped talking and followed me along the corridor.

I was feeling good about where the investigation was going. In one week, I've identified two participants. Now we needed to get a handle on what they were up to.

12

ON THE WAY TO THE HOSPITAL PARKING LOT, I noticed a couple of men hanging around the main entrance. They made me nervous. Didn't look familiar but there was a familiar aspect to their appearance. The off-the-rack suits they wore didn't disguise the pistols and holsters under the jackets. The other give-away was the way they moved. The "gun" arm swung about an inch or two farther from the body than the other. Years of accommodating a weapon gave them the look of ones with concealed-carry permit for firearms. I'm not sure why I assumed a permit; if they are on the other side, the weapons were no doubt illegally carried.

The two made no effort to approach or follow me, so I did my best to put them out of my mind. I did, however, mentally catalog descriptions of the two. The drive home was uneventful and traffic going out I-630 was light. I made it to my condo in near record time.

Inside my home, the blinking light on the phone told me there was a message waiting for an answer. I punched the button and heard Aaron's voice. "Hey, Casey. My flight was delayed and I won't be able to get home before Tuesday evening…late. Did you get in touch with your vet? If not, do it as soon as possible. See you later."

I dialed the number for FBI agent Montgomery Williams looking for a quick update. There was little to tell him other than seeing the two guys hanging around the hospital. He left me with what I supposed was his standard warning, "be careful." How inane was that. I thought of running with scissors or playing in traffic just to spite him. Decided those actions wouldn't help much.

It was past closing hours for Dr. Jay's office. I knew if I called this late, I would get a recorded message telling me to dial the on-call number if it was an emergency. I swore to myself I would call her from work sometime tomorrow morning. I kept wondering why Aaron seemed so concerned about me getting in touch with the vet.

13

I GOT TO WORK ON TIME TODAY. DIDN'T WANT MOLLY to get used to seeing me come in early. When I passed through the parking lot, I saw the same two men eying me as I walked to the main hospital entrance. I took out my cell and punched in the quick-dial for Falcon.

As usual, I got his voice mail. I left a message telling him about the two who appeared to be shadowing me and asked him to check them out. I figure if anyone can learn who they are it would be Falcon.

The middle of the morning arrived before I remembered to call Dr. Jay. She was busy and the receptionist told me she would return my call in a few minutes. I gathered up Janet and we headed for the cafeteria. This was a better than usual cafeteria, they had a coffee bar that made tolerable espresso and lattes.

I found a seat and my phone rang. It was Dr. Jay and she told me we needed to talk about PK. I got a cold feeling and muttered about being busy at work. She said, "Casey, I'll be happy to stay after closing hours and wait for you. About what time can you be here?"

"I suppose I can make it by five-thirty."

Dr. Jay said, "Great, I'll see you then."

Janet and I talked about Mrs. Manfriedy and her involvement. We wondered how many others were co-conspirators and what role she played in the scheme. We made a date to meet here for lunch and massage our information more.

On the way back to the office, Janet excused herself and headed toward a rear door to the cafeteria. It was a shortcut from here to the parking lot. There are plenty of windows and I paused to see where Janet was headed. Before she was out of sight, I saw my two "bad" guys move up on her, one on each side, and herd her around the corner of the building. "That's spooky," I said.

I went back to the office and busied myself with the stack of folders on my desk. I verified several against my copy of a medical code list. All I needed to do was cross-check the doctor's paperwork about the treatment or procedure, verify the codes entered by the doctor's staff and look at my list to see they were the same. Janet returned to the office and went to work on her own stack of files.

I leaned back as if to rest my eyes and thought of the process. The work was a virtual no-brainer, so I wondered what the difference between the files could be. I handled and those locked away in Molly's desk. No answer. I scanned my folders and realized all of them were simple routine procedures. What if? What if you could turn a routine expense into a more exotic one? The more complex the treatment, the more valuable to the doctor and the hospital in billing charges. I began to look for a pattern. If I could come up with a way to accomplish that task we would be off to a running start.

At lunch in the hospital, Janet and I discussed our findings. "Why is Mrs. Manfriedy part of this plot?" I said.

"Her job as the head of Human Resources gives her a wide range of options. Who else can wander anywhere in the hospital without raising suspicion?"

I admitted Janet's point was valid. "Well, that gives her access, but what does she have to do with the fraud?"

We left it there; neither of us had a plausible answer. Heading back to our office, I glanced out the windows by the side door of the cafeteria. The two men I was concerned about were lounging nearby, between the building and the parking lot. Both were smoking, taking long drags and blowing streams of smoke into the air around them. I pointed them out to Janet.

"Guess those two galoots don't know this is a no smoking campus," I said. Janet gave a head shake and a shrug but didn't say anything. That seemed peculiar to me since I saw her with these two earlier.

Before we got back to our office, I dialed Falcon's number for a second time this morning. Voice mail again—so I left a message. "Falcon, this is Casey. The two guys I told you about are hanging around the hospital again and they seem to have an interest in Janet as well. Did you find out who they are? Anyway, I'd appreciate it if you were around the parking lot when I head home. Oh, not home—I need to stop at the vet's office after work."

14

MOLLY WENT ON ONE OF HER USUAL UNEXPLAINED absences. Since it was twenty to five, I decided this would give me a head start for the vet's office. I left the building and started across the hospital parking lot toward my Mustang. My two thugs were on a collision course toward me. As I continued, one was to my right rear while the second guy was coming up on my left.

With a quick glance over each shoulder, I gauged the distance to cover before I reached my car. I guessed they didn't know what I drove or couldn't see it. If they knew, it should have been easy for them to cut the angle and intercept me. I estimated their distance without looking and mentally the time to intercept. I figured I could reach my car twenty to thirty seconds before they overtook me.

With a two-step hop, I grabbed the shoes off my feet and began a sprint to the Mustang. I heard one of them shout something, but I wasn't paying attention. With my key out, I was inside my car way ahead of them. Key in ignition. Crank the engine. Throw the old gal into gear. Stomp on the gas. I checked the rear view as I gunned out of the parking slot and down the aisle toward the exit. The last I saw of them, they were still standing in my recently vacated parking spot and each was shaking a fist at me.

I settled down on the ramp to I-630, slipped my shoes back on and used my cell to call Falcon. I reached him without going through his voice mail. Quite a feat. "Falcon, I just had a run in with those guys I told you about. In the hospital parking lot. I think I could describe them to a police artist."

"Calm down, Casey. I'll get to the bottom of this. Just steer clear of them for another day. Here's another number where you can reach me. It's direct and I'll always answer your call. It's like 9-1-1 to me; can be most places in town under ten minutes."

We chatted for a few more minutes. Nothing about our cases, so I guessed he was giving me time to unwind. I thanked him and said good-bye and he was gone without a reply. Standard procedure for Falcon.

I steered toward the side street on Chenal Parkway just past Shackleford. I was only a few blocks from the vet's office and the apprehension began to grip me. I felt a sinking feeling in my stomach. I was sure Dr. Jay's news would not be positive.

When I walked into the Tail-Waggers Veterinary Clinic, I saw Dr. Jay. She had a smile on her face but I could sense a more serious demeanor. She led me back to a room they have set up as a grieving room. I felt the pressure in my chest tighten and I wondered if I would survive this ordeal. There were tears filling the ducts and in imminent danger of spilling into my eyes. Dr. Jay's eyes seemed damp as well.

She took a deep breath, squared her shoulders and began what I thought was a memorized presentation. Then I realized I was being unfair to her. I'm sure she's been through this ordeal often enough she has found the best way and sequence to present facts to a pet owner.

"Casey, when Aaron brought PK to my office last week, I was concerned with his health. I knew you wouldn't object, so I went ahead with blood work and an X-ray. The blood work didn't show the problem, but the X-ray did. I confirmed that PK has squamous cell carcinoma in his upper left jaw."

"What do we do to treat it?"

"That's what we have to talk about, Casey," Dr. Jay said. She waited for her serious concern to soak in, then continued. "Unfortunately, that location, the upper jaw, is the worse place we could have found the cancer."

Cancer? She used the word I was dreading. "Is there anything we can do?"

"There are interventions…they're radical…and the quality of life following the operation is very likely minimal to nonexistent."

She fell silent and allowed me to absorb what she just said. After a minute or two, she continued, "Casey, we have to look at the alternatives."

"What are they?"

She went through a ton of detail, but it boiled down to letting PK live as long as possible or help him out by easing him into the next level of life—or in this case, death. She said his cancer was aggressive and metastasizing quickly. PK would go downhill rapidly and it would, in all likelihood, be accompanied by pain.

I looked at her hoping she would hold out an optimistic path for me. After minutes of choking back the emotions I was feeling, I said, "If PK was your cat, what would you do?"

"I can't answer that for you, Casey. As much as I would like to help, the decision has to be yours."

"I guess I need some time to think this over."

"I can understand that, but don't wait too long. I believe PK is already feeling the effects of the cancer, and it will only get worse. Here are three papers you can look over. They are non-medical, but some owners say it helps them with the decision."

I glanced at each of the three pages. The top one said something about "the cat 10 commandments," and the second one was titled "Last Night." The final one was called "The Rainbow Bridge."

Dr. Jay handed me her card with a number written on the back and told me to call her as soon as I've made a decision. "Don't worry about the weekend. If you want to see me again on Saturday or Sunday, use the phone number on the back."

Heading to my condo, I drove slowly, slower than my normal speed. I wondered if I would attract police attention moving at such a rate. I didn't want to arrive at home. I knew I would break down as soon as I hit the front door. PK has never presented much friendliness or affection. Recent days have been different. He spends more time hanging around wherever the tenants of his home were. Last week, it was Effie and Aaron who noticed and commented on how PK was slowing down and having trouble jumping up on the furniture. I didn't want to face them and go through Dr. Jay's talk with me.

I slipped in the front door and picked up PK's brush from the wicker basket just inside. PK was there to greet me and I gave him a come-along noise and waved his brush in front of his nose. Though he's not that friendly, he loves to have his coat stroked with the brush. He followed me into my bedroom where I sat on my bed and patted the mattress next to me. PK was on the floor judging the distance up to the bed. He decided it an impossible task and meowed at me. I reached down and scooped him up onto the bed.

I became so involved in my investigations at the hospital, my personal life was on hold. Being jerked back to my home life, there was nothing pleasant to look forward to. I didn't want to face the coming decision, but...

15

IT WAS MIDEVENING BEFORE I LEFT MY BEDROOM. I knew Aaron was still at work and Effie was probably in her room. I still didn't want to see anyone. Not so. Effie was reading a newspaper in the living room. She looked up as I entered.

"There's some supper in the fridge—all you need to do is nuke it in the microwave," she said. "If you feel like talking, I'm here."

Her demeanor was comforting, and her voice so low it was soothing. I began to put this afternoon's events out of my mind. "Thank you, Effie…maybe later." I headed for the kitchen. The ten o'clock TV news ended, and the late show was into the first commercial break after the monologue. The front door opened and there were a couple of plops as Aaron dropped his bags in the entryway.

"How's it going?" he said.

I saw Effie look at me and then to him—she shook her head. *Always the mother hen.*

Either Aaron missed her signal or decided to ignore it.

"Casey, did you talk to Dr. Jay?"

I rose, stalked to my room and slammed the door. Even with the door closed, I could hear Effie castigating him.

* * *

My mood was a bit better in the morning. I apologized to Aaron and Effie over breakfast. I shared Dr. Jay's words with them. They both looked like I was delivering bad news about their own pets.

Effie started three times to say something, but the words didn't come out. At last, she said, "Have you decided what you're going to do?"

Aaron's eyes were moist. "Casey, whatever I can do, I'll be here to help."

"Me too," Effie said.

"I appreciate your sentiments. Now I'd better get ready for work."

16

AT THE HOSPITAL, JANET AND I SPENT AS MUCH TIME as possible discussing the fraud without arousing Molly's suspicions. We debated Molly's destinations on her clandestine trips beyond Human Resources and did our best to estimate how far she could get in the time she was gone. We vowed to time her next trip out of the office.

We were in luck. Not twenty-five minutes later, Molly withdrew several files from her top left drawer and departed. Janet and I each checked our wristwatches. I pretended to focus on my work, but my eyes moved from watch to wall clock and back.

After fifty-five minutes, I looked at Janet and shrugged. She said, "This ain't working. Molly could have walked downtown and back by now."

I nodded. "Next time, we'll have to work out a way to tail her. We need to know what offices and people she sees." With that, Janet and I went back to work in earnest. Another hour passed before Molly returned. She came into the office with empty hands. When she turned her back to us, we each gave a shrug and an eye roll.

Late in the afternoon, I worked up the courage to dial the number at the vet's office. Dr. Jay was busy with a client and the receptionist said she would call back as soon as she was free. I wondered if the word *client* referred to a pet or the owner. I almost hoped she wouldn't return my call.

When my cell rang, I jumped. The caller ID read Dr. Jay. "Hi, Casey. Sorry it took so long to get back. What can I do for you?"

"I just want to let you know I haven't decided yet what to do with PK. Would it be okay to check back with you on Friday?"

Dr. Jay assured me Friday would be fine. She also asked if I was close to a decision. I had to say, "No."

17

I WAS IN A FOUL MOOD THE NEXT MORNING. I WAS testy with Aaron and Effie and their looks didn't ease my mood. PK ambled out to the kitchen to greet me. None of the usual rambunctious racing through the house. I added food to his dish. He sniffed around then ignored it. I reached for the cabinet above his dishes and said, "Treat."

That word usually generated enthusiasm. He loved the brand I found on my last trip to the grocery store. I broke it up into three pieces and put them on his mat. He sniffed, licked one up in his mouth and let it drop back onto the mat. He began a slow trek into the living room.

I did my best to evaluate his condition. Wasn't eating, not even his treats. PK was moving slowly, and he'd lost at least a couple of pounds. I sighed and choked back my emotions.

I needed to get dressed and leave for the hospital. The day would be a bummer leaving him behind. On my way out of the condo, I apologized to both of my roomies.

My attitude didn't change. I found myself apologizing to Janet as well. I saw the two guys I've seen recently headed toward our office. Through the glass door, I saw one look at Janet and toss his head to the side. I took it for a "come with me" signal. I must have been right because Janet rose and hurried to meet them in the corridor.

The men stationed themselves on either side of Janet and hustled her away from the office. I wasn't sure, but I got the feeling her feet weren't touching the marble floor.

* * *

I considered dialing the "9-1-1" number Falcon gave me. I quit holding my breath when Janet returned to our office.

"Janet," I said, "those were a couple of tough looking characters you left with." I paused for effect hoping my comment would elicit a response. Stony silence greeted me. "Okay, if you're not going to talk to me, I'll drag it out of you…Who were those dudes and what did they want with you?"

Janet turned her back to me and began working on a file folder in front of her. I waited a while longer hoping she would open up. Didn't happen.

I gave up and started working on the stack of folders in front of me. By afternoon, my concentration didn't exist. I still needed to make the decision about PK.

Molly was out of the office, so I told Janet I was heading out. "If Molly asks, tell her I had a family emergency."

On the way to my car, I saw the same two guys again. *Damn, I don't feel like a hassle. Maybe they won't try to follow me.* I was in luck. Either they didn't see me, or they were no longer interested in me. I checked the rear-views and was sure no one followed me to west Little Rock.

PK greeted me when I entered my condo. He perked up his head, but didn't muster enough energy to get up and follow me. When I did coax him to me, I watched him closely. He was favoring both his front legs. I offered PK his favorite treat. He sniffed at it but didn't bother to pull it into his mouth. I picked up the treat and held it toward him, which he took this time. When he tried to chew, I saw him wince. It looked like the attempt to chew was painful.

Only one more distasteful chore I need to complete today. I picked up my phone and dialed Dr. Jay's office.

18

THE NEXT MORNING, I SAT ON THE FLOOR BRUSHING PK with his favorite brush. He rolled over showing his belly and then onto the other side. It took me more than an hour to dial Dr. Jay's office and confirm a time.

"Casey, it's probably best if we take care of our appointment this morning. Waiting will only create more anxiety."

We settled on ten a.m. I took a quick shower and returned to PK with the brush. I spent the next half hour sitting on the floor fussing over him. My eyes were so moist my vision was blurred. Even without looking at my watch, I knew it was past time to leave.

While I was fretting over PK, I received an incoming from Becca. "Hey gal, Aaron called me, said I should give you a ring."

She caught me off guard and before I could rein myself in, I blubbered the whole story to her.

"What time ya going?" she said.

I told her I was on my way out the door and she said, "I'll be there." Then she hung up.

With PK's brush tucked into my jacket pocket, I said, "Come on PK. Time for a ride." His ears pricked up at the word ride. I helped him into our soft pet taxi. He was listless and showed little of the pleasure he usually experienced for an outing in the car. Before I pulled out of the garage, I let him out of the carrier. Rather than putting his paws on the window ledge, he laid down on the seat and put his head on my lap. Before he dozed off, PK looked up at me.

Becca met me at the front door to the vet's office and went in with me. She asked the vet if it was okay for her to be there with me. Dr. Jay nodded her head. We followed her into the grief-comfort room.

The procedure was simple and short. I used the brush to help remove any apprehension he might be feeling. Dr. Jay administered the first shot, a tranquilizer to relax PK. He looked at me as the vet inserted a second needle.

I could swear his eyes said, "Thank you." The life faded from PK's eyes and he was gone. I wept and noticed Dr. Jay was crying as well. Becca put her arm around me.

"If you're reaching for anything besides a handkerchief," Dr. Jay said, "we can take care of everything else later. I'll perform a necropsy to verify my previous diagnosis." She and her assistant reached for a small white sheet lying on the procedure table and covered PK's body.

"What about his remains?" Dr. Jay said.

I confirmed that I did not plan on a burial or memorial for PK. Dr. Jay told me she could take care of all the details.

The drive back to the condo took years. I needed to pull to the curb twice to wipe my eyes so I could see the road. At home, I looked around at his belongings; chew toys, bed, blanket and litter box. I didn't have the energy to gather them up. "I'll leave them here for you PK. Maybe next week we can figure out what to do with your things."

I noticed the smell. The aroma of a hospital or of the vet's office was on my clothing and I choked up again.

* * *

I was sitting in a darkened condo when Effie and Aaron came home. I checked my watch and realized I'd been here more than six hours. Both looked surprised when they switched on lights and found me sitting there.

Effie was the first to speak. "For goodness sake, Casey, what's going on?"

I gathered all the courage left in me and told them about the events from Wednesday until now. "I figured I'd have the weekend to recover before I had to go back to work."

They plunked down on the couch, one on either side of me. Aaron said, "Why didn't you tell us? I could have gone with you—at least for moral support."

"Me too," Effie said. "Do you need us to do anything with PK's bed or toys?"

"I'm going to leave everything as is until I know what I want to do."

We chatted a few minutes more and I excused myself and headed for my bedroom. *PK, it's going to be damned lonely around here without you.* I fell into bed exhausted and was asleep in minutes.

19

BY MONDAY MORNING, I COULD THINK OF PK WITH-out bursting into tears. On the way to work, I could almost feel his head resting on my lap.

My cell phone rang and it was Falcon. He told me he would meet me in the hospital parking lot. I saw his car and parked near him. Walking to the building, we both saw the two men who've been hanging around.

As we neared them, Falcon edged away from me. The men stopped about twenty feet in front of us. Falcon kept moving until we narrowed the gap to ten feet.

Falcon was the first to speak. "Show some tin or back off." He eased his jacket open so they could see the 9 mm Sig Sauer nestled in a holster under his arm.

Both men extended their arms with palms toward us. One reached slowly for his jacket and pulled it back revealing a badge. I could see a gold circle with lettering and a five-pointed star filling the center. Without being close enough to read the words, I knew it said: United States Marshall. The second man did the same and the tension eased. One said, "Ms. Fremont, Janet Jordan has something she wants to tell you. Then you'll understand why we've been hanging around."

I walked to my desk. Janet looked at me and said, "You look like you been crying the whole weekend."

It dawned on me I did a slapdash job with makeup this morn-ing. Words exploded from my mouth. "I had to put my cat down last Friday."

"Was that the 'family business' you needed to attend to?"

I nodded. She said, "Fine with me. If anyone asks, I'll tell them you had to bury your twin sister."

"My twin sister? I didn't even know I had one. Thanks."

I smiled and she put an arm around me. "Casey, I have something to tell you. Let's take an early break."

By nine forty-five, I couldn't stand it any longer. I caught Janet's attention, nodded toward the door and got up. Janet followed a minute later.

Seated at a table in the cafeteria, Janet learned forward. "Now you know who the two men are."

"I still don't know why."

"Mysterious meetings. U.S. Marshalls—you must have a guess."

"Okay. I'll guess. I'm not sure there is a Witness Security office here in Little Rock, but I'd say you're involved in the WitSec program somehow."

"You got it. I can't give you any details about who or what happened to put me there, but I am in the WitSec program. There are people looking for me."

"You have my word," I said. "I won't say anything about you to anyone." I thought about my roomies—it would be tough not to tell them. "How come you're telling me now?"

"My handlers did a deep background check on you. They said I could brief you at my discretion." She shifted in her chair and looked over both shoulders. "I suppose you could say we're both undercover."

On the way back to work, Janet and I scouted several corridors Molly could have taken during her time out of the office. Janet looked at her watch and said, "Holy smoke. We've been gone over forty-five minutes. Molly will be dropping bricks out her back side."

"Don't sweat the small stuff."

"Yeah, and everything's small stuff," she said.

20

JANET'S PROGNOSTICATION WAS RIGHT ON. MOLLY was sitting on the edge of her desk drumming her fingers when we walked in. "Where the hell have you two been?"

On the way back, I had time to come up with a plausible explanation. I hoped it would be believable. "Molly, I'm sorry. Janet and I were talking, and I wasn't paying attention. I led her to the elevator and punched a button to go down. Instead of our floor here, I ran us clear to the basement. Did you know the morgue is down there?"

I think the question threw her off stride. She sputtered and said, "Of, course I know it's down there." She shrugged her shoulders. "Now, get back to work and no more screw-ups like this."

Returning to her desk, Molly picked up the phone and dialed. I could tell it was an inside call because she didn't have to dial "9" to begin. Too bad these internal calls didn't have a "last dialed" function. I didn't dare get close enough to hear her conversation. She was already on edge. I wondered if there was any way to determine the number she dialed, and decided there probably wasn't.

Lunch time arrived and Janet and I headed out to a small restaurant near the hospital. Over our meal, we decided it might be time to chill out on our snooping. Janet said, "I got a feeling Molly is so uptight she is about to pop."

"I think you've got it right. What say we take a couple of days off before we resume the investigation?"

We both nodded and began working on the salads we ordered.

* * *

All our good intentions faded when by midafternoon Molly gathered several folders from her *special* drawer and headed out of the office. Janet and I stared at one another for a few seconds and stood in unison. "Guess a little bit of snooping won't hurt," I said.

Janet nodded and we started out the door to our office. "Can you think of any way we can follow her without being seen?" I said.

"We can use the fish-eye mirrors they have mounted at each corridor intersection," Janet said. "If we stay back just far enough to be out of sight, we can see around the corner to tell which way she goes."

"Great, but what if she looks behind her and sees us in the mirror?"

"The mirrors are only there to give people a general idea of the traffic around a corner. They aren't clear enough or sharp enough to make out the features of a person."

We used this technique for three turns as Molly headed for her destination. As we approached the next corner, Molly stopped, turned and stared back and up. It appeared she was using the mirrors as well—checking behind her.

We stopped, half-turned away from Molly, and began an animated discussion as if arguing. Then we turned and went back the way we'd come.

"She still might be able to identify us by our outfits," I said.

Janet suggested we wear scrubs over our street clothing. I thought it was a good idea, but still had a question. "Where the blue blazes do we get a set of scrubs?"

"I can take care of that," Janet said. "Maybe we better put off trailing her until I can get us the disguises."

21

THE NEXT MORNING JANET SHOWED ME THE SCRUBS
we would use to blend in. She took the green set and left the
blue one for me. The outfits were large enough to wear over our
street clothes. She handed me a hair net for my head. "After I got
the scrubs, I thought about our hair color. Even with this new
clothing, Molly might notice a blonde and a brunette following
her," Janet said. "She might put two and two together and think
of us."

Once at our desks, we didn't have long to wait. At nine-
thirty, Molly grabbed a batch of files from *the* drawer and
headed out of the office. We each pulled our scrubs from our
desk drawers, slipped them over our clothes and headed off
to trail Molly.

I felt relatively safe in the disguise. We used the hallway mirrors to keep track of her and stayed far enough behind that she
wouldn't spot us. This tactic worked well for four turns, but then
the bottom fell out. We had dropped further back and saw Molly
make a right turn. This particular corridor was a short distance
to another intersection. Before we could get to the corner, Molly
was nowhere in sight.

We stopped to evaluate the situation. If Molly turned right at
this point, she would be headed toward the accounting department. If she took the opposite direction, Human Resources was
most likely her destination.

"Which damn way did she go?" Janet said.

"Don't know. Could be either way. Got any idea which direction is the most likely?"

We debated for several minutes; Human Resources or accounting? We didn't reach any conclusions. "I think we should get back to the office," I said.

At our desks, we shed our disguises just before Molly walked in. "Whew," I said under my breath. "That was close."

Janet made a grimace and nodded.

Over lunch Janet and I tried to figure out how Molly got back to the office so quickly. She sketched a floor plan of the hospital on her paper napkin. "If she went to Human Resources, it would be a long way back to our office. But if she went to accounting, there are a couple of hallways that would be a shortcut back to the pharmacy."

"Okay, I'll buy that. Now, who can we look at in accounting?"

22

TWO MORE DAYS PASSED WITHOUT AN OPPORTUNITY to follow Molly. Janet and I wondered why she didn't have any files to transport, but we only had speculation.

On Thursday, Molly was not in the office. We learned she was attending a meeting outside the hospital and would be gone until noon.

"If only we could find some of those folders in an office somewhere," Janet said.

I nodded. "Can we wander around enough to look for them?"

We decided to scout different parts of the hospital. Janet said, "You can cover the accounting department; I'll look around the Human Resources area."

We also decided to meet in the cafeteria around ten-thirty. That should allow plenty of time before Molly was due back to the office.

I took the path Molly covered when we lost her at the corridor turn. When I arrived at the corner in question, I turned toward accounting. It was a pair of good size rooms filled with cubicles staffed by busy little bees. I found a clipboard on top of a filing cabinet near the entrance. Near the cabinet were supplies for a copier. I grabbed a half-dozen blank sheets of paper. The wastebasket next to the copier was full of rejected copies. I added a couple of them to the stack on my clipboard.

Nothing like a stranger wandering around a work area with a pencil poised above a clipboard to keep heads down. The usual reaction is to notice a stranger's face, then see the clipboard and the busy pencil and the thought I'd better look busy. It worked like a charm.

I covered most of the area in both rooms without arousing suspicion. I didn't see any file folders I recognized as being from our department. There were a pair of offices, one in each room, with doors and the doors were closed.

I wanted to know what these men looked like and get a look at their offices, but I can't just barge in…Then it hit me; the answer was easy; it's a scene from one of my favorite late-night movies *Three Days of the Condor* starring Robert Redford. I identify with the character Kathy Hale played by Faye Dunaway. She helps a good guy in trouble.

I memorized the names on the doors for the two divisions in accounting; Chet Peterson – accounts payable and Ralph Hodgekiss – accounts receivable.

Clipboard in hand, I barged through the door marked Chet Peterson. Once inside, I looked around the room for a general impression. When the man behind the desk looked up, I said, "Mr. Hodgekiss?"

"No, I'm not Hodgekiss young lady. You'll find him in the office around the corner."

I apologized profusely and backed out of the office closing the door on my way. At the next office, I reversed the names and used the same ploy. I didn't see much, but now I could recognize both men by sight.

By now it was time to meet Janet. We got a cup of coffee and settled at a table far away from other diners. Comparing notes, we found there was little intelligence to report. I said "Guess how I got a look at the guys in accounting," and described what I'd been doing.

"That was a gutsy move," she said.

Janet's report for the day contained even less.

* * *

After work I got a phone call from Falcon and set up a meet. He suggested a small neighborhood bar not too far from the hospital. He said, "They've got a grill and we can get a burger while we talk."

"Wow, you know all the ways to a gal's heart; at least to her stomach." I hung up, found the bar and scouted for a parking place. Easy to do. The paved area behind the building could accommodate a half-dozen cars.

I squeezed in between a large black Jeep and a gigantic SUV, a white Ford Explorer. Falcon was already seated at a booth in the back when I entered. The smell of stale beer assaulted my nostrils and I shook my head doing my best to get the odor out of my nose. We each ordered a burger and a bottle of beer. I asked for "no onions" and Falcon requested double onions on his.

"I guess you're not planning to get close to anyone tonight," I said.

He had a quizzical look on his face. "I mean I suppose you're not planning to kiss anyone." He shifted in his seat and crossed his legs away from me and I could swear his face showed a tinge of crimson, but Falcon is adept at covering any feelings he might have.

We talked about both cases. I told him we didn't have any real suspects, beyond Molly, in the Medicare fraud. He told me the signs of drug theft were getting hotter.

"Anyone in particular you're looking at?"

"Not a single person, but we believe someone in the accounting department must be involved."

I looked at Falcon and liked what I saw. He was good looking in a rough, tough style. I knew he could take care of himself; of course, the Sig Sauer helped. I also guessed he could do quite well in a one-on-one fight—maybe even if the odds weren't even. Since I was a CI and couldn't date Dennis, I decided I'd like to spend some time "off duty," so to speak, with Falcon.

I toyed with the condiments on the table between us and remained silent. That's a good ploy to get someone to rush into the vacuum of silence. Didn't seem to work with Falcon, so I jumped in myself. "Do you want to do anything after dinner here?"

He started to say something but all he did was squirm in his seat again. "Well, I guess we could…could…"

He wouldn't finish the sentence and it was driving me up the wall. I stuffed the last bite of the burger into my mouth. I remember mama telling me not to talk when I'm eating, but I was ready to give up on Falcon. "Well, if you don't have anything else to say, I suppose I might as well go home." He still didn't say anything and I was still munching on my burger as I left the bar.

23

TODAY'S FRIDAY THE THIRTEENTH; I WONDERED IF I could turn it into a positive. I jumped out of bed and hustled to start a pot of coffee. Entering the kitchen, I was surprised to see Effie there already. Don't know why that caught me off guard. Since PK died, neither Effie nor Aaron would let me do anything around the house.

I'd been okay for the last day or two, but the thought of PK's death set me off. I muttered and spun around. I didn't want Effie to see the tears racing down my cheeks. I spent the next hour in my room taking a shower and dressing. It took several applications of a washrag soaked with cold water to reduce the redness around my eyes to the point I felt I could face the public.

I slipped out of my condo without having to see my roomies—well almost. As I reached for the front door handle, Aaron said, "Casey…Casey you've got to let us do something for you."

"Do what? You and Effie won't let me do a lick around here. You're always hovering…" Before he could say a word, I slammed the door from the hallway and started down the stairs to the parking garage.

The word at work was that Janet was out sick with a flu bug, which disappointed me. I wanted to bask in the glow of my forays into the offices of Peterson and Hodgekiss in accounting.

I was hoping we could don our disguises and do more follow-up tracking of Molly. Swept up in the intrigue, I found it difficult to go a day without looking for more information on the fraud.

By midafternoon I found my mind bouncing between PK and Falcon. I did my best to shift my attention away from my cat. Every time I remembered PK, the emotions struggled to surface and the tears were near. *Should I call Falcon or not?* I repeated the same thought several times—no answer came. "At least I'm not hearing voices." I smiled at myself.

"What was that?" Molly said.

"Nothing. I was just thinking of something." Figured I would be better off leaving it neutral rather than mention a person.

An hour later, I told myself, what the hell. I grabbed my cell phone and punched in Falcon's number. As I suspected, I got his voice mail and said, "Falcon, this is Casey; I'm having dinner at Augustinos restaurant tonight at seven-thirty. If you're looking for a date, be there."

* * *

By seven-fifteen, I was seated at a table in Augustinos sipping a Scotch and soda. My eyes alternated between my wristwatch and the fancy wall clock near the front door. I swore the second hand on my watch stopped; it was only two minutes since I last looked. Seven-thirty came and went. I ordered another drink.

The waiter said, "Is Madam ready to order?"

"No, *Madam* is not ready to order yet." I saw a frown on his face as if watching a dinner tip fluttering through the air and out the door. I said, "Eight o'clock and I call it quits."

I was reaching for my purse and getting ready to leave when he said, "Sorry I'm late. Parking around here at night is a pain."

I looked at my watch; seven fifty-six. "You almost missed our date." I saw the crimson creep up from his shirt collar and threaten to invade his face. "This *is* an official date, isn't it?"

The silence was like the inside of a mausoleum. After what seemed like two or three hours, he said, "I suppose you could call it that."

We talked about our cases, both of which were proceeding at a pace a snail could overcome. We talked about ourselves. Falcon was reserved when it came to details about himself; so I carried the conversation.

When I mentioned PK, he kept asking questions about the cancer and the day PK died. There was a look of pain on his face. The same look I saw when we attended the funeral of Raphael de Jesus, a man who died helping us track down Romeo.

"You're really stressed out, Casey. You need something besides the case you are working on to take your mind away."

"Got any suggestions?"

"Well, dating like this gives you a break."

"Does that mean you're going to ask me out again?" He squirmed in his seat and the crimson threatened another take-over.

We changed subjects and began talking about our backgrounds, and what we liked in music. Ex-spouses came up—I was the only one with that history. Again, I gave up way more information about myself than Falcon did.

The next time I looked at my watch it was half past eleven and we decided to call it a night. I left an overgenerous tip for our long-suffering waiter. Falcon walked me to my car. He started to leave and turned; I took his arm, reached up and kissed him on the cheek.

He said, "Goodnight." And he was gone.

24

I GOT TO SLEEP IN TODAY. SATURDAYS ARE GOOD. Janet called; she announced she would be not be coming to work all of next week—the flu was the culprit.

The call surprised me. Why in the world did she go to so much trouble—looking up my number; calling earlier than I would have if I felt lousy with the flu? Why did she care? *Forget it, Casey; it's a weekend, relax and enjoy the time off.*

I dismissed the phone call and moved toward the kitchen. Effie and Aaron were standing in my path, and they herded me to my favorite chair in the living room.

Aaron pointed to the chair and said, "Sit."

I started to say something back to him; some scathing comment like—who died and made you my mother? Instead, I eased into the chair.

The two of them pulled side chairs up in front of me and sat down.

Effie said, "Casey, we need to talk with you and you—"

"Damnit, Casey, this is an intervention." Aaron said. "Effie and I are worried about your well-being. Ever since PK died, you've been in a brown funk…and that's three shades worse than a blue funk."

That almost brought a smile to my face. Instead, I said, "Whose damn business is it anyway? Maybe I like the funk I'm in."

"You know that's not true," Effie said. "You need to stop blaming yourself. It was a cruel fluke of nature. You didn't do anything wrong. You couldn't have treated PK any better or any worse—the outcome would've been the same. You didn't cause the cancer; you couldn't have cured it."

I sat up in my chair. "Okay, are you two through now?"

Aaron leaned forward, his voice well above his normal conversational tone. "Damnit, Casey. Pay attention. You've got to get some outside activities to help you help yourself. I've seen people with less of a problem decide to kill themselves."

"What sort of damn *outside* activities should I get?"

I started to say more, but Aaron held a hand up, palm out to silence me. He said, "You haven't even picked up PK's litter box, let alone his toys and blanket."

"I don't *want* another pet."

"Then how about some useless and impossible cause to champion," he said.

"Alright, I'll try to find something."

"In the words of the Jedi Master, Yoda, 'do or do not, there is no try.' Don't *try*, Casey, do it," Effie said.

A smile did it's best to curl the corners of my mouth.

Aaron leaned forward again. "I need you to give me your word on something."

"What?"

"Before you do anything that might harm yourself, promise you'll call me."

"I guess I could do that. Where did you get that?"

Aaron said, "Once upon a time, I had to make that same promise to my counselor."

"Why were you seeing a counselor?" Effie said.

Aaron looked at both of us. "That's as much as I'm willing to share…for now."

* * *

In the middle of the afternoon, I was feeling frustrated that I wouldn't be able to do any snooping at the hospital. One person alone was more apt to draw attention, and Janet would not be there with me. Then, one of those light bulbs over my head snapped on. Becca was the answer.

I called and set a meeting with her. I told her about Janet. We agreed to meet at the same bar Falcon took me to.

"So, what you got in mind?" she said.

"I need some help at work to push ahead on my investigation. See you at the bar."

As I left my condo, I told Aaron I would remember his admonition and repeated the promise.

Becca and I settled in at the bar and ordered a draft beer each. After the waitress left, we got down to business. We worked out a cover story for Becca, and went over a set of signals we could use to pass information or warnings.

With our hospital business out of the way, we chatted about recent events. "I gotta tell you, Aaron called me and asked how you were doing," Becca said.

"I think he's overstepping his place."

"Hey, girl, be careful how you word things. Remember I'm black too."

I realized how my words must have sounded and felt worse.

"Look here girl, he's worried about you. And from what he told me, I'm worried too. You gotta get a grip."

I found myself leaning away from Becca and fidgeting in my seat. "Damn, I know something is wrong and I don't know what to do about it."

"Go with it. Believe in your friends and listen to them. We only want what's best for you…but you gotta do the work and make the decisions."

I found tears running down my cheeks. Becca took my hand in both of hers and just held on. "We all love you, Casey."

"I know. I know. I'll take what all of you have said seriously and pull myself out of whatever I've fallen into."

We agreed to meet at the hospital on Monday morning and get to work on our latest mystery.

25

I LOOKED AT THE PAPERS STREWN ALL OVER THE living room. "There sure isn't much in a Sunday paper these days," I said.

All I got were head nods and grunts in response to my insightful comment. "Okay you guys, what's up?"

Effie jumped to her feet and announced that we were all going out for lunch. "C'mon Casey, let's get dressed."

"What's the hurry? It's only nine and we can't eat this early."

"Quit arguing," Aaron said. "We thought we'd do some sightseeing on the way."

"Sightseeing? What in the world is there we haven't seen in Little Rock?"

Aaron stood up. "Why do you have to be such a pain in the ass, Casey?"

I caved and was at the front door in thirty minutes, saying, "Okay you guys. I'm ready, where are you?"

* * *

After what seemed like a waste of time and not seeing anything new, I said, "What's the big surprise?" Silence from the front seat. I looked around to orient myself. We were northbound on I-430 and Aaron took the Colonel Glenn Road exit. He hung a left from the ramp onto Colonel Glenn Road. In a few blocks he pulled into the front parking area of a business. I was shocked when I read the sign: Humane Society of Pulaski County.

"Damn," I said. I told you I wasn't ready to replace PK."

Effie turned in her seat to face me. "We know. Aaron and I've been looking around and thought you might like to see someone we met."

It took one of them on each side to herd me up to the door and into the shelter building. The sign on the front said they opened at eleven a.m. I looked at my watch and it was only ten-thirty. "Guess we'll have to come back some other time. They're not open."

"That's okay," Aaron said. "We made arrangements with the staff to let us in a bit early this morning."

The woman sitting behind the front desk acknowledged Effie and Aaron and then said, "The young lady you want to see is in Room 1." She nodded toward her left.

We entered to find the "young lady" was no more that a teenager. She introduced the pup that sat in her lap. Seeing us, the dog jumped down and came toward us wagging its tail so hard the whole back end followed the wags. The girl said, "She's sort of a Yorkie-poo with a bit of something else mixed in."

I found myself squatting down to get a better look at this small bundle of energy. She was a medium black with a light brown muzzle. "She? Is this a female?"

The girl said, "We think she will be the size of a Miniature Poodle and weigh around ten pounds or so when she's fully grown. Is that too big for you?" The look in her eyes seemed to say, please say yes, she's too big.

We got the whole story. This girl was providing a foster home for the dog. When she was adopted, the girl would take on another charge and go through the entire process all over. Take one home, bond with the animal only to have to relinquish the pup to others.

"We worked out a name for her," Effie said. "Aaron came up with it. We can call her Sergeant York, 'cause she's a Yorkie, at least partially. Aaron told me Sergeant Alvin York was a hero and one of the most decorated soldiers in World War I. We can shorten it to Sergeant. How's that?"

"So, you two have it all worked out, have you? Who's going to clean up after a dog? What makes you think I want a female? I'm used to a male cat."

They stumbled all over each other issuing assurances that they would help. "We even have a supply of pads to help house-break her," Effie said. "And Aaron and I have done our share of scooping PK's litter box."

"Okay," I said. "I'll go along with a trial period. If she doesn't work out, I'll bring her back."

I saw a brief look of hopefulness on the face of the lady who fostered the dog. It faded as my new charge moved close to me and allowed me to pick her up.

And so it came to be. I was sitting in the backseat cradling a squirming dog who was intent on liking my face off.

Back at home, the dog was struggling in my arms so I lowered her to the carpet. She ran around the house exploring and looking like she wanted to mark her territory, which meant urine on the carpet.

She disappeared down the hall and when I located her, she was squatting in PK's old litter box. She left a sizable wet spot in the litter, climbed out, cocked her head and looked at me. I knelt down and said, "That settles it little girl. You are now an official member of this group."

26

ON MONDAY MORNING, BECCA AND I PARKED NEAR
enough to each other we could maintain visual contact. She
was ahead of me and moving slower than she usually did. I
picked up my pace and moved around her. As I did, she said,
"See you inside."

When I reached the lobby, I stopped to rummage in my purse,
allowing Becca time to catch up so she would have no trouble
following me. I took the most direct route to my workplace, and
as planned, I walked straight to Molly's desk and said "Good
morning." She looked surprised, muttered a response and went
back to work.

I glanced out the window to the hallway and saw Becca run
a hand through her hair—the signal she understood and knew
what Molly looked like. She moved farther down the hall and
I lost sight of her.

I felt a cold chill when Molly left the office with a stack of file
folders. It was all I could do to restrain myself; I wanted to jump
to my feet and follow as well. I knew Becca was on the job; now
all I had to do was wait for a report from her.

I found myself going over and over the same case file. I hope
Becca is being more productive this morning than I am. Giving
up on my work, I headed to the cafeteria for a break.

Rounding a corner, I saw Becca coming down the hall toward
me. A large man escorted her—one with an air of authority.
Becca's face was turned toward him, totally ignoring me. Just
before we passed each other, she used the hand opposite her
escort and gave me a thumbs up gesture. It was a positive signal
and yet I wondered who the guy was.

Becca was waiting near my car when I left work. She got in, and I said, "Did you find anything?"

She shook her head and said, "I was pretty sure Molly made me. Couple of times she stopped short, reversed direction like she was looking for someone behind her. I kept walking and went past her without breaking stride. She eyeballed me hard with a look on her face that said, 'do I know her?' but didn't press it."

"Should we back off the surveillance for a while," I said.

"Let's stay with it, at least for another day because the time is ticking by. We've got 'bout two months left until our deadline. I'm not sure it means anything, but Molly went into the accounting department. When she came out, she was carrying more folders than she took in. After that, she headed to Human Resources."

"So who was the guy I saw you with in the hallway?"

"I think Molly called security and he showed up. He couldn't prove anything, so he escorted me to the lobby and let me go."

27

THE NEXT MORNING BECCA CALLED. "I GOT AN excuse for being in the hospital. A guy I know is there for gallbladder surgery. If I'm stopped, I can say I'm there to visit him and bring him some toiletries."

It sounded plausible. As long as they don't dig too deep, it might work.

When I arrived at my desk, Molly was busy sorting folders on her desktop. She accumulated a small stack of four or five, slid the rest into a drawer and locked it.

I saw Becca lurking in the hall outside our office. She was carrying a small bag.

Molly left the office with Becca following at a discrete distance. Alone again, I did my best to picture Becca trailing Molly. At worst, she would give me another update after work.

The assurances I gave myself didn't ease my mind. I was squirming in my seat to the point the case file open on my desk seemed to swim before me. To keep my eyes from crossing, I pushed back and reached for my cell phone.

First, I checked Falcon's number. Voice mail as usual. Next on my mental list was Dennis. Same result. Two for two, bad batting average. "I'll try Effie. She'll answer." I looked around the empty workplace. It was strange being the only one in the office.

I punched in Effie's number. It rang for a solid three minutes and I hung up. No voice mail, and I was oh for three.

My cell rang and it startled me. Caller ID said Becca. I snatched it up and answered. "What's going on, girl?"

Becca whispered. "Can't talk long, gotta go. Meet me in the cafeteria. Don't acknowledge me—I'll leave a note for you—five minutes."

She must have been taking lessons from Falcon, because all I had on my phone was dead air. My watch said half past eleven. Time for a noon break anyway. I scribbled a note to tell Molly I was at lunch.

When I arrived in the cafeteria, Becca was nowhere in sight. I grabbed a paper cup, filled it with iced tea, paid for it and headed for a table. As I sat down, Becca materialized. She headed my direction and dropped a crumpled piece of paper near me. Shuffling along, she kicked the note under my table.

I checked everyone in the room and satisfied no one was watching me, I let my napkin slip off my lap. As I picked up the napkin, I palmed the note. Holding it in my lap, I smoothed it out, and read it without bringing it up to the table.

I could feel the color drain from my face as I read it. It said: *ploy failed—security man and buddy following me—I'm blown—help!*

The adrenalin began pumping and I raced through a list of options. Nothing sounded good.

28

IT HIT ME…I PULLED MY CELL PHONE FROM A POCKET and hit the speed dial for Falcon. When his page came up, I pressed the Text symbol and typed 9-1-1.

He was on the line in seconds and I could hear the engine of his car revving. "What do you need Casey?"

I explained our situation and Becca's note. I heard his car downshift into a full acceleration. "I'm on my way to the hospital," he said. "If Becca is blown, we may have to assume the same for you. Be ready to secure butts and haul ass."

"You have such a way with words." I heard the beginning of a chuckle before his phone went dead.

I headed back to the office when another of those large security knuckle-draggers intercepted me. "C'mon with me," he said.

He was also a mouth-breather, and I would guess his IQ was in the single digit range. I could feel fingers digging into my upper arm, so I didn't resist. His grip on me was strong.

We reached what I assumed to be the security area in the basement. The fact there were no signs on the walls or the door bothered me. Becca was there glowering at her captors saying, "Like I told you a dozen times, I'm here to visit my friend."

Molly was there as well. The burly guy with the vise grip looked at her and said, "Is this the broad you wanted?"

Molly nodded her head, then turned to Becca and said, "Who are you and how do you know this woman?" Her arm went straight out, pointing at me.

Becca put on her most indigent expression. "I told you, I'm a visitor…and I don't know who this white bitch is. Never saw her before."

Molly's head swung toward me. "Casey, how do you know this lady?"

I shrugged my shoulders and remained quiet. I was wondering where this conversation of denials was going. I cocked my head from side to side and gave Molly another shoulder shrug.

The door burst open and I saw Falcon standing there. He pushed his way into the room and wedged himself between my captor and me, then moved toward the other men in the room. He pulled a wallet from his pocket and flipped it open. Light reflected off the shiny badge he produced. He said, "Gordon, FBI—I'll take charge of the black woman," and pointed at Becca. The badge wallet was already back in his jacket pocket.

Molly and the security men were muttering and sputtering. Every one of them was trying to ask questions and protest. The burly guy Falcon detached from my arm lumbered toward him. I saw the man put a hand on the butt of his pistol and challenge Falcon. The hand came out with the gun. Falcon stepped into him, gripped and twisted the man's wrist. His gun clattered to the concrete. The man followed his gun to the floor whining about a "*broke hand.*"

Falcon leaned over him and said, "Try something like that again and a broke hand will be the least of your worries."

I smiled, almost giving myself away.

Falcon took Becca by the arm and escorted her to the door. He said, "Be cool lady, or you'll leave in handcuffs." Over his shoulder he said, "And thanks for the assist in apprehending this woman." A second later he and Becca disappeared down the hall.

After a half hour of verbal sparring, they *released* me and I started toward my office. Thinking better of it, I decided it was time for lunch. I settled on a salad topped with shredded cheese and dressing.

When I returned to the office after my meal, Janet was at her desk. "I'm back and ready to go again on the tracking," she said.

"Janet, I think we'd better cool our jets. I don't want you to get into trouble on my account."

She turned her back on me. Seemed like an unusual action; could she be feeling left out of our surveillance agenda?

My phone vibrated and the noise startled me. I brought it to my ear. Montgomery Williams, my FBI handler, announced himself. Before he could get another word out of his mouth, I said, "Don't ever call me. If I feel the need of a white knight, I'll let you know. Now, get off the line and meet me at the restaurant at six-thirty." I heard sputtering and the words "what restaurant" as I punched the END button. I figured even a Feeb could figure out which restaurant. There's only one where the two of us have met.

* * *

I decided on a fashionably late arrival. When I walked through the door, Williams and Dennis occupied the same table where we met the first time. Dennis was against the wall and the FBI guy was sitting on the aisle leaving the opposite bench open for me. I walked to the table and stuck an index finger in Williams' face. "Don't you ever call me again. I just got out of a scrape and don't need anyone screwing up my work. When I need to talk to you, I'll initiate the call."

"But you're overdue to report in," he said.

Dennis backed him up and admonished me for not reporting on time. "I know you're undercover, but if we don't hear from you, we tend to think the worst."

"I've been preoccupied," I said.

The Feeb said, "What is more important than this assignment?"

"I had to kill my cat…" It was a crude way to put it, but I was tired of these two criticizing me.

Dennis drew back with a surprised expression. "PK?"

"Yeah, PK. He was suffering from cancer." I let it hang there and decided not to tell them about the replacement, Sergeant York.

29

I ARRIVED HOME AND FOUND BECCA THERE AS I expected. I unlocked my front door and said, "Let's get a glass of wine and go over what happened today."

"Now, you're talking, girl. My mouth feels like I've been chewing sand."

We settled into comfy chairs in the living room. I pointed to Becca and said, "You first."

"Well, things were going well until just before I called you. I'm confused about that Molly Rasmussen person. She seems to be working with that lady in Human Resources. She goes there with folders but seems to leave with the same number. On the way back to your office, she loses me. Don't know where she goes between Human Resources and your office."

"You got any idea which way she heads?" I said.

Becca reached for her glass and took a healthy sip. "No. Once I tried to get in front of her—to see which direction she takes. Didn't work. Wherever she went, she didn't come by where I was waiting."

"That's not much help is it? How did you get caught?"

Becca squirmed in her seat. "I'm sorry about that."

"No need to be sorry. We got through it with nobody the wiser—I hope." I leaned back to enjoy the rest of my wine.

"Hey," Becca said. "There was something that struck me...I saw that gal from your office, Janet, head out and since Molly didn't seem to be going anywhere, I followed her instead. She headed to Human Resources, too. You got any idea why?"

I shook my head. "You didn't tell me how they caught you."

"Not sure. I guess Molly saw me in the hallways once too often."

"My fault," I said. "You should have company when you are shadowing someone." Becca was quiet, so I said, "Did I ever tell you where to look when following a suspect?" She shook her head. "Keep an eye on their feet. If the suspect suddenly turns and looks at you, they won't find you staring at them."

"Girl, you just chocked full of bright ideas. I think you misspent your youth hanging around shady characters." She displayed a big toothy grin and took a large sip of wine. "And by the way, how the hell did he show up?"

"I called him and said we needed some help. Yeah. I do know a batch of offbeat characters."

"Offbeat for sure. One of the most outstanding in that category is Falcon. You and him getting it on?"

Becca caught me so off guard, I think I blushed. Her all-knowing nod told me my face was turning red. The phone rang—saved by the bell. I punched the Speaker button. "Talk to me," I said.

A voice boomed from the instrument. "Hi, Casey. This is Alex."

I was totally lost. "Alex? Alex who?"

"I always hated the 'Uncle' label, but would it help if I said; Uncle Alex?"

Becca was giving me her "what the hey" look, so I gave her my stage-whisper. "He's my Mom's brother."

"What did you say Casey?" he said.

"I'm sorry, you're on speakerphone and I was updating a friend about who you are. It's been a long time Uncle Alex. Why the call?"

"I'm going to be in Little Rock in a few days…I thought we could get reacquainted…"

"Sure," I said. "Give me a call when you're in town and we can have dinner."

"Sounds great. I'll do it."

The phone went quiet. When I asked if he was still there, nothing but silence. I looked at Becca. "Do all men have such poor phone manners? Alex is just like Falcon." I was sorry I mentioned Falcon; it might remind Becca of her last question before the phone call.

I breathed a sigh of relief when she said, "Who the heck is this guy, Alex?"

"Like I told you, he's my mother's brother. I heard stories about him and what happened in the 70s and 80s; some wild adventures. Maybe we can get him to tell us what he used to do."

"Sounds good. Where were we?" Becca said.

"Looks like we have a direction, but no verifiable facts." I sipped my wine.

"Molly seems to be working with Rasmussen from the pharmacy, but are they tied to the Medicare fraud? Could be something else," she said.

"Don't forget about the accounting department. You trailed Molly Rasmussen toward accounting. What's she doing there?"

We stared at each other for several minutes. "Enough of this for tonight," I said." My head's getting fuzzy from the wine. Stay over for the night and we can discuss it further in the morning."

30

BECCA AND I MANAGED TO MAKE IT THROUGH THE morning without talking about the hospital and the folks we suspected. Effie joined us for lunch and I began the discussion with Becca. Effie listened but did not participate.

We covered the now familiar ground we talked about yesterday. Effie was leaning forward with her elbows on the table. She was like a fish being reeled in.

"I can help," Effie said. "If nothing else, I can spell Becca following the hospital staff."

"I appreciate the offer, Effie," I said. "But I think Becca should stay away from the hospital for a bit."

Effie nodded with a pained expression on her face. I did a double take when my cell phone rang. I didn't recognize the number of the call but answered any way.

The conversation was short—a couple of grunts, a reference to Augustinos, a muttered okay and a see you there. I pressed the OFF button and found two faces staring at me, eyes wide and expressions that said, Who? What? Where?

"That was my Uncle Alex. Guess he wasn't real forthcoming when he called yesterday." Neither Effie nor Becca said a word. "He's already in Little Rock and we're having dinner tonight."

* * *

I met Uncle Alex at a restaurant I like for good Italian food. We drank Chianti and stuffed ourselves on ravioli.

"Casey, can you call me Alex instead of *Uncle* Alex? The uncle reminds me how old I am."

"You got it. What are you in town for?"

Alex squirmed in his seat. "I'm trying to touch base with the family…"

"You aren't sick, are you?" I surprised myself—not usually so blunt.

Alex explained he wasn't ill, just melancholy and wanted to see family. "I plan to see your parents when I leave here. They're still in Indianapolis, aren't they?"

I nodded and thought about his words. Alex didn't seem like the melancholy kind. His story didn't ring true to me. "So, Alex, what's the rest of the story? The real one."

"Well, I hear you're involved in some nefarious activities." He winked and grinned. "Thought I might be able to lend a hand with your investigations."

If I were Plastic Man, my jaw would have hit the thick carpeting. A thousand questions flooded my brain. I opened my mouth, but the words stuck somewhere between the gray matter and my lips. Alex let me stew in my own juices, until I choked and sputtered. "How the hell do you know about that?"

"Let's leave it this way. I still know a lot of people in agencies usually known by their acronyms—FBI, CIA, NSA to name a few." He let that much sink in before he said, "How about it? Could you use an old warhorse who misses the excitement?"

"Did FBI agent Montgomery Williams tell you about me?"

"Not directly, but when I contacted his boss, he told Williams to brief me in."

"Alex, Williams is a loose cannon on the gun deck. He doesn't know when or how to contact his informants. He's going to be the death of us all."

Alex leaned forward. "Cut the kid some slack, Casey. I know his family and his superiors say he's got talent, even if he doesn't always know how to use it."

"Okay. Just hope he doesn't stick our collective feet in a pile of horseshit." Alex gave me a crooked smile, but he didn't say anything. The waiter brought my spumoni and I dug in. "Don't you want some dessert?"

Alex patted his stomach. "Gotta watch my girlish figure."

I told him I heard the rumors about his exploits and asked him about them. He shook his head and said, "I'm not quite ready to publish my memoires. But that doesn't mean I won't do it."

"I think I remember that your wife died about 1979 and your son went missing about the same time. And a few years later you worked in the Pentagon and the White House."

"That's about right. Maybe before I leave, I'll tell you something about those days."

The look on his face told me he was drifting back to a time back in the day. "I'd enjoy hearing about your adventures, but there's no pressure. Now, is there another reason you are here?"

"I'm looking for something that will raise my blood pressure. At least before they put me out to pasture.

"You're not that old," I said.

"I'm pushing Social Security time. Just not ready to retire."

We talked more about the hospital. I looked down and saw my spumoni was turning into a rainbow of liquid in my bowl. We agreed to meet tomorrow to further discuss my current activities. I gave him directions to my condo and we left the restaurant in separate cars.

31

PAPERS STREWN AROUND THE LIVING ROOM TOLD the story of a usual Sunday morning. I looked at my watch; eight minutes to go. Alex was due at ten a.m. I raced around giving the area a lick and a promise before Uncle Alex arrived. Have to remember to drop the *uncle*. The doorbell rang three minutes later. Peeking through the peephole, I saw Alex standing in the hall. Aaron was approaching from the elevator.

I pulled the door open and Alex started through with Aaron close behind. Alex spun to face Aaron and took an offensive posture. Aaron dropped his flight bag and tensed his muscles.

"It's okay, Alex. This if Aaron Kincaid—he lives here too."

"Sorry, young fellow, didn't know Casey ran a coed dorm."

Both men relaxed their postures, reached toward each other and shook hands. I introduced Alex to Effie and Becca.

"Any more folks lurking around?" Alex said.

I shook my head. We sat down, and I began to cover my experiences over the past month. Sergeant York decided it was time to put in an appearance. She came around the corner and into the living room at somewhere around Mach One. She dutifully stopped at each of the people sitting there and sniffed everybody's shoes in turn. She spent a little extra time with Alex and deemed him acceptable. Having satisfied herself, she did two 360 degree turns and plopped herself onto her circular pillow cushion.

When I felt safe there would be no more dramatic entrances, I returned to my story. "…and that brings us up to last night when I had dinner with Alex."

I did my best to pry some history from Alex, but he remained quiet on that subject. He suggested we get to the business at hand—those disreputable activities at the hospital.

When he arrived, he carried a small over-the-shoulder bag and now he dug into it. He produced four brand-new two-way radios, still in their original packages. He handed one to Becca, Effie and me. "Here, Aaron, you take this one," he said. "I didn't realize I'd need five. I'll pick up another tomorrow morning."

We spent the next half hour getting the radios ready to go; loading batteries, setting the same frequency and practicing. Next, he produced an earpiece for each of us. "This looks like a typical phone headset-transmitter and receiver. They're voice activated, so no button to push—just talk and listen. Enough people use them, so I don't think we'll be conspicuous."

We coordinated assignments for tomorrow and ordered Chinese take-away for supper. Over noodles, pork, chicken and beef, I spent the rest of the evening wheedling information from Alex.

With a look of exasperation, Alex said, "Casey, if you stop trying to pull teeth, I promise I'll show you everything that happened to me in the 70s and 80s.

"You'll *show* me?" I said.

He winked at me as he rose and left the table. Inside two minutes, he was out the door. I stood there wondering about his comment.

32

ON MONDAY, EFFIE AND ALEX SPENT MOST OF THE
day learning their way around the hospital.

The next morning, in my workspace, Janet and Molly seemed
intent on current tasks. Then, I watched Molly pull folders from
her *secret* drawer and leave the office. When she was gone, Janet
said, "Want to follow her?"

I said, "Nope. I've given up on that project."

Janet said, "Well, I'm going." As soon as Janet cleared the
door, I was on my radio. I alerted Alex and Effie the two were
on the loose. I went back to the stack of work on my desk, but
my head wasn't in it.

I left my office for a morning break. When I returned, Molly
was back at her desk. I glanced around as I passed and got a
surprise. Molly is a typical unorganized person at work. So I
was taken aback to see six or seven pencils on her desktop—they
were aligned like a row of soldiers with the erasers in a neat line.
I also got a faint whiff of…something.

A few minutes later, Janet got back from her trip to wherever.
As she passed my desk I caught an odor. Sometimes the hospital
sponsors vendors of books, cosmetics and the like, and they set
up in a meeting room near the cafeteria. I thought Janet must
have tried some perfume and fell into the bottle.

I was about to pass both actions off as happenstance when
I leaned back in my chair and gave myself a mental smack on
the forehead. *Now I'm sure who is coordinating this whole mess.*

* * *

By eleven-twenty, I couldn't stand it any longer. Janet was back at work, but Molly was absent again. I slipped out of the office and made a call on the radio. My cohorts were heading for the van where Becca was overseeing the activity.

In the van, I said, "Give. What did you two find out?"

Effie took the lead. "I followed Molly while Alex stuck with Janet. Molly parked her butt in Human Resources—Manfriedy's office. No contact with anyone else I could identify. She spent some time in accounting, the accounts receivable department I think. Her contact may be Ralph Hodgekiss."

Becca beat me to the next question. "What is she doing in an accounting department?"

"They might use accounts receivable to cover payments received by the hospital," Alex said. "If a payment comes in that isn't from a legitimate billing, Hodgekiss, the accounts receivable manager, could divert it to an account of their own."

"Wouldn't an audit show the Medicare payment discrepancies?" Effie said.

"When it arrives, it never appears on the hospital's books, and I doubt Medicare has the personnel or time to track and cross-check every payment they make," Alex said.

"How about the doctors?" I said.

Alex continued his reasoning. "Probably use fake names for some and crooked docs to cover the rest. In those cases, the doctors are no doubt billing for services never provided." He turned to Effie. "What did Molly do when she was with Manfriedy?"

"Not very interesting for us," Effie said. "She went directly to Manfriedy's office and closed the door. I could see into the office through the window between the office and the ante-room. They were busy talking. Janet was taking notes and went directly to the accounting department when she left Manfriedy's office. I keep picking up rumors about drugs missing."

"I got those same vibes," Alex said.

I held up a hand and said, "Hey, guys. I think I can verify your findings and both the fraud and thefts go straight to one person." That got their attention. I told them about the pencils in Molly's office. "Only one person is that anal retentive, and it's Harriet Manfriedy, and there was a faint odor of that horrible perfume she wears."

"That's one side of the equation. Who's on the other side?" Alex said.

I took center stage again. "I can confirm what Effie saw. Janet Jordan came back to our office reeking of perfume, and it was the same stuff Manfriedy wears. Even though she only spent a few minutes in the HR office, the smell stuck to her like white on rice."

We split up, and I started back to my office.

* * *

As I walked down a long hallway, a man fell in beside me. He was tall, thin with a mustache and a tool belt slung over one shoulder.

"Ma'am, my name's Sam Atkinson. You're Casey Fremont, aren't you?"

"That's right, but I'm not looking for a date right now."

He laughed so loud he looked around as if to see whether anyone was within earshot. "Me neither. My job lets me go everywhere in the hospital, and I pick up all sorts of information." He hitched the tool belt farther up on his shoulder. "For instance, I know you and a black lady got in trouble for following folks around the building. Next I hear you got some people working with you. Am I right so far?"

I started to answer but held back. Is he someone who can help or is he fishing for evidence against me?

"You seem to be well informed. What else do you know?"

He stopped, looked around, then said, "I know I can get in a batch of trouble talking too much." With a foot on the arm of a nearby chair, he busied himself with a bootlace. "Ever hear of Gloria Sexton?"

I knew she was the one who worked in the pharmacy under Molly Rasmussen. I also know she's dead—went off the hospital roof. "I'm not sure. What about her?"

He still looked nervous as he fussed with the lace in his boot. "Around here, you can get dead talking to the wrong person."

His voice was a bare whisper now. "She asked me if I could find out what was going on in the pharmacy area where she worked. I asked around—but before I could get back to her, she went off the roof of the hospital."

"What do you mean, she *went off* the roof?" I said.

"The bosses are pushing the suicide theory. But in light of our talks, I doubt she took her own life. The day she died, she was talking about a weekend trip she was planning with her kids."

At last, with the bootlace cinched up, he put his foot back on the floor. "I been doing a lot of talking. I hope you're on the same side Gloria was. If not, you're probably talking to a dead man."

"I think we're on the same side."

"How many people you got working for you?" Sam said.

I looked at him for a moment, then made a decision. I said "I think we're on the same side; I didn't say I trusted you yet…Bring me something I can use and I'll revisit the trust department."

He hitched up his tool belt again, turned around and moved back down the hallway.

33

THE NEXT DAY, WEDNESDAY, WAS A LOT LIKE THE previous one. Following, coordinating, confirming what we already discovered. We believed we knew who worked with who…we were missing the *what* and *how*. What was each of them doing and how did it fit into the Medicare fraud and the drug thefts?

Maybe I could put Sam Atkinson to work on that end. He gave me his cell phone number when we met yesterday. I dialed and when he answered, I said, "You got a minute?" When he said he did, I outlined what I knew and asked if he could try to fill in the blanks. Sam said he would, but there was a note of apprehension in his voice.

I snatched a piece of paper and began to create an organizational chart. With all the characters we were tracking, I found it confusing. I put Harriet Manfriedy at the top of the sheet. By her name, I wrote "chief, human resources." Next I divided the blank space below her name and labeled the left side "Medicare fraud" and below that, "drug theft." Opposite "Medicare fraud," I listed "Chet Peterson, chief, accounts payable." I put the head of accounts receivable, Ralph Hodgekiss, opposite Peterson. I figured they are on the same level and were connected directly back to Manfriedy.

Toward the top, I printed my boss' name, "Molly Rasmussen, chief of pharmacy admin." I drew a dotted line from Molly to Manfriedy, figuring Molly works with Manfriedy, but probably wasn't directly connected to the two men in the accounting department.

That left me with two questions. I didn't know who the mastermind was or how they managed to fleece hospital authorities.

I sat back and looked at the schematic, and it began to overwhelm me. How in hell can I bring down this many people? I knew I wasn't alone, but even so, the task seemed insurmountable.

Before I left for home, I called Sam and outlined the areas where we were weak. Only, I didn't use the plural pronoun. Best if I keep him in the dark for the moment.

* * *

The full team straggled into my home around seven p.m. I briefed the group about Sam and his possible help. Alex surprised us with ID badges copied from the one issued to me. Once he had mine as a model, the counterfeits were easy for him, or for the people he knew. He gave each of us a list of places in the hospital the badges would take us…and the areas that would be off-limits. For example, we could not access the shipping and receiving area, the dispensing part of the pharmacy, or the storage unit for drugs. "If you need access to any of those areas, you'll have to find another way…or bluff your way in."

Effie said, "How did you get our pictures?"

Alex smiled and said nothing.

I wondered if Sam could cover these areas for me. I tried his number again but it went to voice mail. I left a message to see me tomorrow during my morning break.

With *business* out of the way, we spent the rest of the evening wine tasting. "If we keep having these get-togethers here, I'll need to restock my wine cellar." What I just said hit me. "That was crass of me. I didn't mean it to sound like I was asking for donations."

There was a chorus, in unison, saying, "Yeah. Right."

* * *

We all sat quietly sipping wine.

"Casey, what's with the thousand yard stare?"

I shook my head to bring myself back to the table from wherever I was. "Guess my mind was wandering."

"Where were you?" Alex said.

I shared the concerns and the weight of the odds against us that occurred to me this afternoon.

I showed the group the diagram I created earlier. "If anyone has more, or sees an error, please make a note on the drawing." I waited a couple of minutes while the paper circulated around the group. "There's already five names on the list and a couple of slots with no name attached. That's more than a half-dozen…I'm not sure I want to take on those kinds of odds."

"Look," Alex said, "we've probably all had at least some of those feelings. What we have to keep in mind is to take it one step at a time."

"Like eating an elephant?" Effie said.

"Exactly," said Alex. "One bite at a time."

I steered the group back to the job at hand, and we resumed our discussion about the hospital.

"How do they get away with stealing drugs?" Effie said.

Alex sat up. "As I understand it, they can write off a certain amount as *spoilage*; that is, ruined during shipment. Extreme temps or water damage is a plausible cause. I bet if we check the hospital's records, they would show well over the average for spoilage. All those drugs go to them for resale. If that doesn't provide enough for them, they might substitute fake pills for real ones."

"Alex, can they fake enough spoilage to make it worthwhile?" Effie asked.

He referred to some notes and said, "You're right Effie. In addition to delivery problems, they can fake dates on current stock. Drugs have an expiration date as well as a beyond-use date. If they fudge the dates and certify destruction, they can move a lot of drugs from inventory to their profit."

"What do you mean *certify*?" Effie asked.

Alex glanced at his notes again and said, "The hospital has an incinerator that qualifies for drug destruction. Really, all they need is a furnace that burns over twelve-hundred degrees centigrade. I know they have federal concurrence to destroy drugs as long and two department heads sign off on the destruction. Part of our investigation should be to find out who is signing those documents."

"My hunch is Molly Rasmussen is one and the other signature is the head of HR, accounts receivable or accounts payable," I said.

Becca leaned forward. "How do you counterfeit pills?"

"They don't produce them. They look for cheap pills that are substantially the same size, shape and color. They may pay a dime for a generic and sell them as the real pill for ten dollars or more."

I looked at Alex. "How do you know some much about stealing drugs from hospitals? Have you been on the inside of similar schemes?"

"I used what little I know of hospital operations and applied intuition and logic to fill in the blanks…and I got lucky on a couple of forays around the hospital. We need to confirm the *who* and *how* they do it. Otherwise, all we have is this supposition, and the authorities will never act on our ideas."

Before we wrapped for the evening, we set up a meeting for the coming weekend. We would include Aaron in our task force.

34

AT WORK THE NEXT MORNING, I FOUND MY MIND wandering again. So much for my workload. I looked forward to tomorrow, Friday, because Aaron would be returning from a weeklong stint in the air. He should have several days off and we could certainly use his help. It would also give us the whole weekend to integrate him into our investigative group.

It dawned on me that Aaron wouldn't have an ID badge. I hit a number on my speed dial and hoped Alex would pick up. He did. I told him about the missing ID badge.

"Come on, Casey, give me some credit. I created a badge for Aaron and I'll deliver it over the weekend."

He rang off, and I was alone again. The image of my diagram of crooks flashed in my mind. I wondered if what we had was right. Who are the rest of the conspirators?

"Casey!" The voice startled me. I looked around and saw Molly staring at me. She said, "If you don't have enough work to keep you busy, I can shove another pile to you."

I buried my head in the folders on my desk and cranked out a pile of folders that threatened to flood my Outbox. Next, I spent my morning break contacting my "team" and inviting them to my home on Saturday to flesh out what we knew about the people at the hospital. Falcon was the only one who would not be there. He begged off saying other commitments needed his attention so he could put some food on his table, reminding me his contributions were pro bono.

I managed to concentrate enough to reduce the pile of fold-ers on my desk to three. It was close enough to lunch time; I decided to leave them for the afternoon. After a quick lunch in the cafeteria, I roamed the halls.

I thought of my perpetrator diagram and the offices representing the people involved in the crimes. I pulled a copy of the drawing from my pocket.

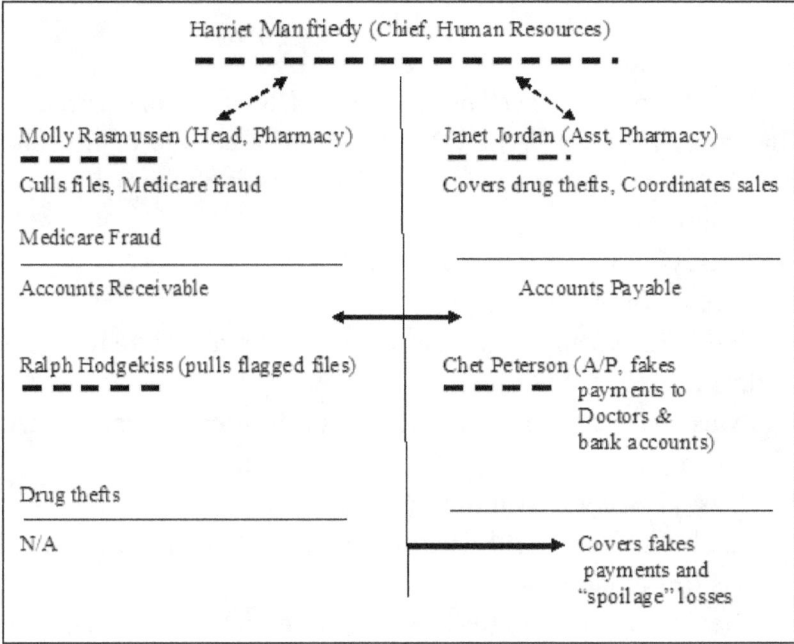

We were investigating Harriet Manfriedy in HR, accounts receivable's Hodgekiss, and Patterson from accounts payable… Adding my boss, Molly and Janet Jordan rounded out the Medicare fraud side of my drawing.

The drug theft part of the diagram was blank. We needed to concentrate on that part of the crimes. By the time we're done, I bet there'll be a dozen names on the list.

* * *

Friday was much a repeat of yesterday. I marveled the woman I replaced could turn this into a full-time position. Maybe her intellect was on the low side, or perhaps it was just the opposite. She was drawing down a sizable salary for a position requiring little effort, mental or physical.

* * *

Midafternoon, my cell phone vibrated. Surprise of surprises— the caller ID read FALCON. We spent a couple of minutes chitchatting before his voice went lower and the tenor sounded more serious.

"Casey…Are you busy tonight?"

"No. Is something wrong?"

"Nothing wrong. I was just wondering if you'd like to go out to dinner."

I was so surprised; my mind went into mental brain freeze. It took me so long to reply, Falcon broke in.

"Casey? Are you still there?"

"Yeah. I'm here. And…is this so we can talk investigations? Or…Is this a date-date?"

There was much sputtering from his end, but few intelligible sounds. Then he said, "I don't think of myself as a dater, but…I suppose you could call it a date."

I smiled to myself; a *man of the world* flustered like that. "Fine. What time will you pick me up?"

We completed time and restaurant details. He mentioned, "Agustas." I asked if he meant Augustinos. A quick, "Yep," and the discussion ended.

After work, I headed west toward my home. I decided to stay off the interstate so I could enjoy the ride on surface streets. The skies were clear and the temperature was moderate. I stopped as I exited the parking lot and put the top down on my Mustang.

I took Markham and passed the headquarters of the Little Rock Police Department. I hadn't seen Dennis in days. I wondered if our "love life" was still alive. That led to Falcon. There was a big question mark by his name. I enjoyed his company, but aside from a dinner out there wasn't much recent activity. Should I make a move and call him more often?

* * *

Aaron wasn't home when I arrived. I told Effie I of my plans for dinner and told her she should go ahead without me. I did my best to steer the conversation away from my dinner plans—to no avail.

Question upon question and I finally said, "Okay. I'm going to dinner with Falcon."

A smirk and multiple eye-rolls greeted my announcement. I decided to give her my silent stare. It didn't work. I began giggling like a schoolgirl. "So, it's been a long dry spell. What about it? I don't see you to getting out and around." The two of us dissolved into near hysterical laughter.

At half past seven, I headed down to the lobby of my building, and a "maybe date," but I wasn't about to ask Falcon to pick me up at my door. Falcon was waiting at the curb with the engine idling. I got in and saw that even a "date" didn't alter his wardrobe. He was wearing his usual black clothing—head to toe. As I eyed his clothing, I mentally compared it to what I was wearing. Nothing fancy, but the colors of my slacks and shirt and blouse were varied, not the same drab shade. I like bright hues that match or contrast. I thought today's combination tan shirt jacket, cranberry blouse over beige slacks made a statement. We filled the silence with idle chatter as he headed for Augustino's restaurant.

* * *

A waiter approached our table. "Good evening," he said. "My name is Paddy and I'll be your server tonight. May I bring something to drink while you look over our menu?"

I checked his name tag; it read Paddy, so at least he was honest so far. Falcon ordered Scotch whisky straight up, then he looked toward me and asked me what I'd like to drink.

"A white Zinfandel, please."

The waiter jotted our drink order on a small pad, handed us menus and headed for the bar. I couldn't put my finger on it, but Paddy seemed to be hanging out in another world.

We checked the menu, and compared possible dinner choices. I was leaning toward a veal dish, while Falcon was adamant about the spaghetti and meatballs. "Oh, come on. Italian restaurant and all you can think of is spaghetti and meatballs," I said. "Surely you can expand your taste buds beyond the standard fare at an Italian eatery."

The waiter returned balancing our drink orders on a tray. As he bent to transfer the drinks to our table, I noticed liquid on his tray which no doubt came from sloshing glasses before delivery. The tray wasn't the only thing that was damp—perspiration covered our waiter's forehead. I thought his demeanor unusual. Like most restaurants in the summer, the air-conditioning was set too high for me. I shrugged deeper into the jacket draped around my shoulders.

I was about halfway through the glass of wine when Paddy placed a baked ziti appetizer on the table. I reached for a bread stick, my third I think and munched away while shoveling in the ziti. I didn't realize how hungry I was until Falcon gave me an eye roll and leaned over the table. "Slow down, Casey. We've got all night."

I laughed, leaned back and slowed my chewing. Might as well enjoy the taste rather than gulping it down. "I love being with you. You don't mind telling people what you think." He looked at me with puzzlement on his face. I couldn't think of anything to say, so I winked at him and went back to my ziti and bread sticks.

We talked more as I enjoyed the appetizer and my eyes roamed the dining room. Over Falcon's shoulder, I saw a pair of women being escorted to a nearby table. One took her seat immediately while the other gestured, said something and walked toward the rest room area.

A few more minutes of discussion with Falcon and I noticed the same woman returning to her table. She stood behind her chair, bent over and placed the inside of each elbow on the outside of the chair back. Using this elbow grip, she slid the chair back a few inches so she could slip into the seat without touching anything. I think I was grinning—

"Casey, what the devil are you doing?"

"Sorry…I was off in the ozone somewhere." I described the woman's actions and we both laughed—not loud enough for anyone else to hear.

Our waiter passed by the table and told us that dinner would be out soon. Falcon excused himself and headed toward the kitchen area. I figured him for a limited bladder.

I was looking around for Paddy so I could get a refill for my wineglass. My gaze landed on the TV set over the bar as the "breaking news" tag caught my eye. There was a long shot of the Little Rock airport with smoke and flame visible. A trailer at the bottom of the screen told me a Boeing 737 crashed on landing.

35

AS I STARED AT THE TV MONITOR, MY CELL RANG, and I checked the ID. "What is it, Effie?" I said.

"I just got a call from the airline Aaron works for. I guess he listed us as emergency contacts. All they said was the plane he was on slid off the runway and was heavily damaged when it spun around—"

"What does *spun around* mean?"

"I don't know, Casey. That's all they said."

"Did they tell you what hospital he was taken to?" I said.

"From the gist of the call, I think he is still at the airport. Are you going to the airport?"

"You bet your bippy. Can you make it over here to the restaurant? That'll save time."

"I've already called a taxi; be there in twenty minutes or so." With that, Effie rang off.

I looked around for Falcon; he seemed to have disappeared. I started toward the bar when I saw Paddy exit the kitchen and head for our table. Falcon was close behind him. *What the hell was he doing in the kitchen?* He was looking at me with his head cocked to one side, a perplexed expression on his face.

"We've got to get to the airport. Aaron was in a plane crash. Effie is coming here, she'll ride with us." We both reached for our wallets, but Falcon was faster. He tossed three fifty-dollar bills on the bar and said to the maître d', "Emergency. Got to leave. That's for dinner, drinks and a tip." He also dropped a business card on top of the bills. "Give me a call if that doesn't cover the tab." On the way to the front entrance, we passed Paddy, our waiter.

Falcon kept his eyes straight ahead and said in a voice only loud enough for the waiter and me to hear. "Make the phone call we discussed; I'll touch base with you later tonight."

* * *

We only waited about fifteen minutes for Effie to arrive. We saw her cab approaching and she exited the vehicle at the front door. The three of us climbed into Falcon's car and started for the airport.

At times like this, I wished I was in my Mustang, driving rather than riding with Falcon. I wasn't sure his car had the brute force of my little Ford. I soon learned what the car may have lacked in oomph, Falcon's driving skills put us out front.

I noticed he ran about eight miles per hour over the speed limit. As if he were reading my mind, he answered my question. "I'm banking on the fact nearly every police officer will give away five miles-an-hour. A quick tap on the brake and I can be down to the speed limit before the radar gun can register me…I hope."

Falcon eased around the curve approaching the airport terminal and pulled onto the curb and stopped. We piled out and moved toward the entrance. A police officer approached waving us back toward our car. Falcon put an arm in the air with a badge in his hand. "Emergency," he said and kept walking. The policeman seemed confused but did nothing further to stop us.

Security was all over the airport lobby. I wondered how we were going to learn anything and get to the survivors' location. I neared the first line of defense and said, "We have to get to wherever the people from the plane are."

"Sorry, lady. Can't let you through. Only family is allowed past this point."

"I'm looking for a crew member. His name is Aaron Kincaid." All I got was a repeat of his previous admonition.

He repeated his warning for the third time. Oh, epiphany…"I'm his wife and these two are with me."

"Well, then. Why didn't you say so first?" With that, handed me three badges displaying a large "V." "Go on down to the baggage claim area; there are people there who can give you more information."

"Wife?" Effie said.

I shrugged my shoulders and gave her a wide grin. "C'mon, let's get down there."

I couldn't believe the chaos on the lower floor of the terminal. The large baggage carousels were still and silent. The din of voices more than made up for that quiet. Crude hand-lettered signs dotted the area and I searched for one that might point me to a source of information. The one reading "Families" seemed to be a logical choice. Pointing to the sign I said, "Let's give that one a try" and led the group through the crowd and toward the sign.

A lady in a TSA uniform appeared to be in charge; if anyone can be in charge of a mob. To me, it looked like herding cats would be easier. "Excuse me," I said. "Do you have any information on crew members?" Without giving her an opportunity to reply, I added, "I'm looking for Aaron Kincaid…he's a flight attendant on the plane that crashed."

Lady TSA flipped through pages on a clipboard, running a forefinger down each sheet before going to the next. She scanned the last page and said, "I don't see his name. You did say he was a passenger, didn't you?"

With pursed lips and rolling eyes, which I did my best to conceal from Lady TSA, I said, "Noooo, he is a flight attendant, a crew member."

"Oh," said Lady TSA. She looked around her cluttered work area and finally shuffled another clipboard to the top of the stack. One that read "Crew." Since this was a much shorter list compared to the passenger manifest, it only took her a minute or so to gather the desired information. Mainly to herself, she said, "Charleston…Douglas…Ferguson…Morelli…No, I don't see a Kincaid on the list."

She dropped her head and refused to look me in the eyes. "Look again," I said. "He called us before takeoff to let us know he was inbound to Little Rock. Look again."

Lady TSA, with her eyes still downcast, said, "There were two people who died in the incident, and their names were removed from my lists."

I felt the world crash down on my shoulders and my eyes filled with tears. "No, it can't be."

Effie put an arm around my shoulder and I let the tears flow. Falcon leaned over the makeshift desk and rummaged through the various clipboards. He raised one that was headed, "Deadheads." He took TSA Lady by the arm and said, "These are crewmembers too, aren't they?"

Lady TSA snatched the paperwork from Falcon's hand and said he was correct. She flipped open the cover and ran her finger downward. "Kincaid," she said, "His name is here."

"Where would he be?" Effie said.

"If he was injured, he was probably transported to the hospital. If he's okay, the survivors are further down the hallway." She pointed over her shoulder and we thanked her as we left.

I saw a man in the uniform of the airline Aaron works for and headed his way. "Excuse me, I'm looking for Aaron Kincaid."

"This here area is for family only," he said.

"I'm his wife."

"Who you trying to fool lady? I know Aaron, and he's gay."

"So, I lied a little." I pointed to Effie and said, "The three of us are roommates and I don't think he has a family; at least not here in town."

"You Casey Fremont?"

I did a double take wondering how he knew my name. "Yes," I said.

"Well, why didn't you say so? You're the lady detective he works with. Talks 'bout you all the time." He took me by the arm and motioned for Effie and Falcon to follow him. "Aaron's in this office area."

He left us alone and I opened the door to the office he indicated.

Effie said, "Aaron!" She shouted loud enough to attract the undead whose hearing is notoriously poor. He was just inside the door and we swarmed him.

We peppered Aaron with questions until he threw up his hand. Only one hand since the other arm was resting in a sling. He said, "I'm fine. Got banged around a bit, but no real injuries. Can't say anything about the accident…er…incident…company policy. And they don't like using the word accident."

We stopped the inquisition and let hugs do our talking. From Effie and me at least; Falcon remained at the back of the pack, not participating in the glad-handing. We, Effie and I finished, and Falcon did step up to shake Aaron's hand. "Glad you're okay, young fellow," he said.

36

WE GOT A FEW HOURS SLEEP BEFORE WE reassembled in the kitchen. Aaron was off for the weekend and said he would also be free for the next week waiting to testify at the National Transportation Safety Board inquiry. We enjoyed breakfast together. The smell of eggs and bacon frying added to the ambience.

After we each rummaged through the newspaper, we gathered at the dining room table to discuss the next week's activities. Becca called, and when I told her of our plans, she said she would be here in thirty minutes. I answered the doorbell and Falcon came in saying he figured our merry band would be plotting for the week ahead.

"How much time have we got left until that deadline?" Becca said.

I looked at the banner on the paper for the date. "There's six weeks to go."

The plan remained the same for Becca, coordinating from our van in the parking lot and for me, doing what I could from my desk inside to help direct operations.

Aaron would participate as a patient wandering around looking for his doctor. Falcon was to show up in disguise since several people saw him when he liberated me from the hospital goon squad. Effie was due enough time off to participate for most of the week. Alex would be a roving member ready to fill in when needed.

The consensus was that we would keep Janet Jordan in the dark about our actions. Even though she helped me in the early stages, I was no longer comfortable with her.

The office routine was the same boring effort. Pick up a file—verify the name—verify the procedure—put the folder in a new stack—start over with the next folder. I kept waiting for a two-way radio buzz to alert me to a call. The Bluetooth device in my ear would allow me to carry the conversation as long as I kept my voice low. I was fortunate; the nearest occupied desk was about fifteen feet from me.

On the way to a restroom break, I noticed Effie and Aaron loitering nearby. I frowned at them wondering where Falcon was lurking. I spotted a staff maintenance man pushing a trash cart carrying a broom. I thought of Falcon, but the bad posture and the gray hair under the ball cap threw me. I was accustomed to seeing him dressed in black, but when I caught his eye, I knew it was Falcon.

I settled back in at my workstation. Molly left her desk and said, "I'll be gone for a while." She was carrying a stack of about ten folders.

I pressed the transmit button and said, "Team. This is Charlie. Molly's on the move." To keep from using our actual names on the unsecure radio, we decided to use the phonetic alphabet based on our first names. The only conflict in first initials was Aaron and Alex. Aaron became Alpha One, while we assigned Alpha Two as Alex's code name. In response, I heard, "This is Alpha Two, I'm on it." I knew Alex would be occupied for the next half hour. Becca chimed in. "Bravo here, I copy."

"Team, this is Charlie again. Looks like Janet is headed out of the office as well."

"This is Echo. I've got this one."

The morning and afternoon went pretty much the same. I tried to keep track of the folders being shuffled around by Molly, but that became too complicated. I gave up, figuring we would check the details at home tonight. By four p.m. the activity slowed to a crawl.

* * *

After work, we had a brief discussion on the radio and agreed to reconvene at my condo. Once everyone arrived, we decided it might be more productive to record our daily logs and compile them at the end of the week.

That effort took only a few minutes and we found ourselves staring at one another. The nonproductive interlude was interrupted by a trail of barking which started in my bedroom and ended when Sergeant York bounded off a chair seat and landed on the dining table where we were gathered.

In her short stay with me, I discovered she was a super sound sleeper. I also discovered when I found her asleep, she needed to be wakened in a gentle manner. The first time I startled her from a sound sleep, she went straight up in the air, turned to face me and was barking before she hit the floor again.

I was thankful she didn't inherit PK's habit of racing into the living room and bouncing off the trompe l'oeil mural and crumpling to the floor. I miss my old psychotic, PK the cat.

* * *

I was excited when Friday night arrived. During the week we emailed reports to everyone covering our daily activities. Effie volunteered to compile them. And tonight, we would combine and analyze our results. Last Wednesday, I ordered a huge whiteboard and a box of dry erase markers which Office Depot delivered the next day. Wonder what my neighbors thought about that humongous board sitting outside my door on Thursday.

Now it was time to get to business and pin down our adversaries.

37

OUR DECISION TO LEAVE JANET JORDAN OUT OF THIS past week's activities was a good one. Turned out she was a busy beaver all week long and I was glad when this meeting on Friday evening arrived.

Before everyone arrived, I placed a set of the emails, a legal pad and pens at each place around the table. I also included a wineglass and when all the guests were present, I produced a bottle of Chianti and one of white Zinfandel. We used the pass-it-around and serve yourself method to select our choice of red or white. The final addition consisted of several small bowls of chips and pretzels.

The usual chatter ensued as we seated ourselves around the table. An enticing aroma emanated from the kitchen—something Effie put in the oven a few minutes ago. Sergeant York upped the noise level by welcoming each person to the table then racing around its circumference until she met the next arrival.

Effie opened her notebook and began to list the group's activities.

* * *

We set ground rules. Each would read from their emails, so they could amplify if needed. Effie pointed to me for the first input. Before I picked up my stack of paper, I said, "I need to update all of you about someone. I think most of you know about Sam Atkinson, a hospital maintenance worker."

I looked around the table and got several affirmative gestures. "Sam has been nosing around for us. I asked him to help look for drug thefts. I heard from him on Monday, Tuesday and Wednesday morning. We planned to meet midafternoon on Wednesday. He was a no-show and I haven't been able to contact him since." I paused for breath and swallowed hard. "I am afraid something has happened to him. When I went to the cafeteria on Wednesday to meet him, of course he wasn't there. One of the cashiers stopped me, checked my ID badge and told me Sam left a note for me." I could see the eyes of everyone around the table riveted on me. My hunch was that the same thought had occurred to each of them as well. *One of us is missing and probably dead.*

I read Sam's note aloud: In a rush. Think they may be on to me…Following this intro was a list of people, departments, and in parentheses after each entry, his best guess as to the person's role in the drug thefts. I looked around the table and saw somber expressions on each face.

Alex leaned in and said, "I think the highest priority of our group for next week should be finding this Sam person." Everyone muttered a *Yes.*

By ten p.m., we had a good list on the white board. I divided the board into two categories—Medicare fraud and drug thefts. Although we had to make a few assumptions, we felt confident about the overall scheme.

I did a recap for my cohorts starting on the left side of the white board. "My co-worker, Janet Jordan, is deeply involved in the drug business. She's covering up the thefts and coordinating sales; although she does not seem to be involved in the Medicare fraud aspect. My supervisor, Molly Rasmussen, culls the fraudulent cases and delivers them to Human Resources. Harriet Manfriedy, the head of HR, is up to her eyeballs in both the fraud and thefts. Molly and Janet both report direct to Manfriedy, but through separate channels. I doubt they were aware of the other's involvement."

As we guessed earlier, we were now certain many of the drug shipments were faked. Large amounts of "spoiled" drugs were pulled and identified for destruction. Rather than incinerating them, they shuttled the drugs to an unidentified group of "salespeople." On the fraud side, Ralph Hodgekiss, head of accounts receivables, was in a position to intercept fraudulent income and shift it into accounts the group controlled. Fake payments were shunted to doctors engaging in the phony procedures using the same bank accounts set up for the perpetrators by the chief of accounts payable, Chet Peterson.

"What do we have we can take to the cops? I mean, all we really have are suppositions," Aaron said.

I waved my stack of emails in front of me. "I think we have a reasonable case at this point in time. They can't expect us to have extensive hard evidence for the position we're operating from. If we had search warrants and full police authority, we would have enough to hang them by now." I looked around, but nobody had anything to say. "I have a meeting with Dennis and the Feeb in the morning. I'll ask them what more they think we can do."

"If that's it, let's get back to the wine," Alex said.

After we were well into the semi-hard stuff, I offered everyone a place to stay for the night. Becca and Alex both accepted. I brought bedclothes out to the living room so Alex could bunk on the couch. Becca and I would share my room.

38

THE WEATHER WAS MISERABLE SATURDAY MORNING.
A throbbing head due to last night's wine didn't help my
disposition.

One of Effie's fixer-uppers—scrambled eggs with a bit of hot
sauce, bacon and hot coffee—did wonders for me.

* * *

It was midmorning and time to leave for our meeting with
Dennis and the Feeb.

The trip to my car was a chinch since I park in a covered
garage. But…the excursion from the parking lot to the restaurant
would be enough to soak us through. I had a rain slicker but
all I could offer Alex was an umbrella. "It'll have to do," he said.

The roads were slick with standing puddles everywhere. On
the freeway, I hit a patch of water and felt the Mustang try to
veer as we hydroplaned on the surface of the liquid. The rear
end began to come around to the right. I steered that direction
and we had just enough traction for my correction to avert a
real problem.

"Nice control," Alex said.

We hummed along I-630 eastbound. I was supposed to meet
Dennis and FBI Special Agent Williams at an obscure restaurant
out past the airport. I eased into the exit ramp for I-440 and took
the center lane. I decided to hold my speed five miles per hour
under the limit. A couple of minutes later, Alex said, "Casey.
Black SUV coming up hard on your right. Keep an eye out."

I recognized the gold medallion on the grill. The Chevy SUV loomed large in my mirrors, and he was hugging the line between his lane and mine. *If he holds there, he's going to sideswipe me… or worse.* He was about five feet from my back bumper and he still held his line. I jinked left, took my foot off the gas pedal and the SUV nearly overtook us. He decelerated and dropped back moving more into his own lane. "Alex, what do you think?"

"I think he's definitely going for you—maybe trying for a PIT maneuver. You did a great job avoiding him. If he comes at us again, see if you can time it so we drop behind him and take an exit."

I checked ahead and saw the next ramp to the right. At the last minute I slid my foot off the accelerator and hit the brake. The SUV stayed with me—his front bumper even with my right rear quarter panel. I didn't think I could shake him. "I'm fresh out of ideas, Alex," I said.

We clicked off a couple of more miles. I tried alternately easing off on the speed and increasing it. Same, same.

"I have an idea," Alex said

39

I LOOKED TO MY RIGHT AND ALEX HAD AN automatic pistol in his hand and was lowering the passenger window. He held the weapon low next to the door side panel where it was not visible from outside.

"Here's my plan. Begin accelerating, and when I yell *stop*, I want you to stand on the brakes. We need to get that SUV alongside us for a second or two. When you hear the gunfire, get back on the gas—hard, and at the same time jump into the left lane. If I can hit his left front tire, he'll be out of the game. We also need to avoid the SUV's swerve to the left. With any luck, we'll be on our way without a shadow…are you ready, Casey?"

"I'm ready." I hit the gas pedal and we picked up about ten miles per hour. My left foot was hovering over the brake pedal.

"STOP."

I stabbed the brakes with all the strength in my left leg. The automatic roared twice and I hit the accelerator and pulled the wheel to the left.

I looked at the rearview mirror and watched the Chevy SUV dragged left by the flat tire, glance off the center divider and begin to fishtail. He was still in view as I saw him maneuver right and pull off into the emergency lane. "Good shooting, Alex."

From the corner of my eye, I saw Alex drop the magazine from the gun and take bullets from his pocket. He refilled the clip and shoved it back into the butt of the automatic. "Thanks. I think I got him with both rounds," he said.

I was glad the rest of the journey was uneventful. After the trip we experienced, the walk in the rain from the parking slot to the restaurant seemed trivial.

We entered the restaurant wet but grinning at each other. "Nothing like a car chase and a gun battle to make you hungry, right?" Alex said.

We made our way to the last booth in the place and slid into the bench seat. I introduced Dennis and Montgomery Williams. The Feeb said, "Didn't know you were bringing a boyfriend along."

"Can the crap, Williams," I said. "Alex is my uncle and he's been helping us."

"I didn't vet him. Please keep in mind I'm running point on this job and if something or someone goes wrong, it's my neck hanging out."

"It won't be me," Alex said.

Dennis reached across the table, shook Alex's hand and said, "Good to meet you. Shall we get to the business at hand?"

"Before we do that, let me tell you about our trip over here," I said. Then I covered the chase in minute detail, except for the gunshots.

"Did you see the people in the SUV?" Dennis said.

I shook my head. "Dark tinted windows, couldn't see inside, only shadows. Best I can say is there were two of them and by their size were most likely men."

"Tried to get the license plate number, but it was covered with mud...couldn't read anything," Alex said.

"That brings us to a rather delicate detail that Casey skimmed over," Alex said. He told them how we evaded the SUV. Williams' mouth was hanging open; Dennis just grinned.

Alex continued. "Dennis, I wonder if you could keep an eye out for accident reports and slide any mention of gunfire into the back of a file drawer." I rather doubt the occupants of the SUV—I think it was a Suburban—will complain to the police, but an alert motorist may have heard the sound of gunfire."

Dennis nodded and I pulled out the paperwork I brought with us. It took twenty minutes to cover everything. When I finished, I said, "How far will this go toward a conviction?"

Williams straightened in his seat. "This looks like a good start, but…I doubt if we even have probable cause to pursue it directly."

"What the hell *do* you need? How about catching them with a hand in the drug drawer? Would that be enough?" Alex said.

Williams sat up straight in his seat. "Hold on there, Buckaroo."

Dennis and I exchanged eye-rolls. The Feeb was doing his best imitation of John Wayne, but he didn't pack the gear to get the job done. *There I go…trying to do my own imitation. Best drop it.*

"Okay," Williams said. "Let's start over, shall we? What we need is actual paperwork that ties the individual to the action."

"Do you mean the real papers involved? We can't do that without giving ourselves away," I said.

Williams explained that photo images authenticated by a reliable person would suffice. He talked about using the cameras built into smart cell phones. The ubiquitous use of phones covered the surreptitious actions. He added one last caution: "Don't forget to turn the flash off on your phone. Nothing like a bright light to draw attention to what you're doing."

Williams explained that he needed images of the paperwork as they moved from one individual to another; time and date stamps from the phone would cover that requirement. They also needed documentation for each image corroborating the date, time, and location in the hospital where the pictures were taken.

The morning was gone and the early afternoon hungries were beginning to gnaw at me. Since we were sitting in a restaurant, I decided a lunch was in order. My Feeb "handler" excused himself saying he needed to get back to his office. Dennis chatted with us for a few minutes while sipping his coffee, then he left using the same excuse.

Alex slid out of the booth and took a seat on the opposite side of the table. "No use banging elbows while we eat." He waved toward a waitress and made a gesture with his hands like opening a book. She arrived with a pair of menus and refilled our coffee cups.

* * *

On the way to my car outside the restaurant, I found myself casting furtive glances in all directions.

"A bit nervous, Casey?" Alex said.

"Guess I'm still jumpy. I'll get over it."

The ride to my home didn't produce any untoward events. I'll admit I breathed a sigh of relief when I parked in the condo's garage.

Back at home, we found Aaron's culinary expertise was put to use as he prepared a meal for Becca, Effie and himself. I marveled at his skill with an arm in a sling and was sorry we ate at the restaurant. His meals were always better than eating out. Both Aaron and Effie were way better in the kitchen than I was. Unless you needed a kettle full of hot water.

The five of us gathered at the dining table once more. I went over our trip to the restaurant. After more than my share of ooh's and ah's about the SUV, the group was silent. Next, I covered the instructions from my FBI agent. That created a firestorm of questions, most of which I guessed at the answers. Alex carried the conversation when I faltered and did a good job of covering my lapses.

When I told the group, the FBI wanted images of documents and how to get them, everyone pulled out a cell phone. For the next hour, we practiced getting a clear image of a single document. The objective was not only to get a good photo, but also to do it so no one nearby would notice what was happening.

Each of us took turns taking single photos by ourselves. Afterwards, everyone had an opportunity getting the photo, while the rest of the group watched and added suggestions.

By ten p.m., I was out of steam. I wandered through a shower with Sergeant York maintaining a constant vigil outside the shower stall. She did her rear-waggling, tail wagging when I exited.

I skipped much of my nightly ritual and collapsed on top of the comforter. Becca nearly flipped me off the bed when she threw back the covers. I don't think I moved a muscle after that until the sun was streaming into my bedroom.

40

WE SPENT MOST OF SUNDAY PRACTICING WITH OUR phone cameras. Around noon, we paused for lunch and turned the TV to local stations to check the news. A breaking story caught our attention—reporters were covering another death— the third, at Little Rock General Hospital. They were speculating whether three people going off the roof of the building was a coincidence.

"Did they mention the name of that person who died at the hospital?" I said.

Everyone shook their heads. Effie said, "They did say it was a man."

"Listen for a name," I said. "I'd be willing to bet it was Sam Atkinson."

Even straining ears didn't give us the answer. The standard "name withheld until next of kin notified" was as close as they came. The only other clue was from one reporter who said the dead man was part of the maintenance staff at the hospital.

We went back to our practice with cell phones. Aaron had an advantage over the rest of us. He used his arm sling for cover and could maneuver the camera freely behind the sling.

We clicked our way through most of the afternoon, then we moved on to a discussion of the three dead bodies and who might have been driving the SUV that came after me yesterday.

The only pair of men we could think of were the two U.S. Marshalls who watch over Janet Jordan. We couldn't make any sense of why Marshalls would act like that.

The next item on our agenda was the man, Sam, and the two women—Roberta Blackwood, an accounting employee, and Gloria Sexton from the pharmacy department—who committed suicide. The discussion became heated. The group expressed various opinions on whether their deaths were suicide or murder.

"I haven't seen or heard anything to indicate they were murdered," I said. "I asked Dennis about it and he didn't have anything to refute the coroner's decision: *apparent suicide.*"

"If they didn't kill themselves, how do you get someone to jump off a roof?" Aaron said.

"I'll track down the autopsy reports," Alex said. "Maybe something in the paperwork will give us a lead."

* * *

Monday heading home, I swung onto the I-630 ramp and settled down at a speed just above the limit. A couple of checks in the rear and side mirrors showed nothing of interest behind me. I was going over the events of the weekend and today in my mind. My eyes returned to the rearview mirror. "Where the hell did you come from?"

A black SUV was hovering a car-length behind me. The gold emblem on the grill was the same; I assumed it was the same Chevy Suburban from Saturday. I repeated the question in my head. I thought I was being vigilant, but the dark behemoth arrived without my seeing it.

I moved from the center lane to the one on the right to check the SUV's reaction. Rather than changing lanes with me, he accelerated. With the Suburban's right rear door next to me, I kept my eye on the front tire and saw it snap to the right. To preserve the custom candy-apple red paint job on my Mustang, I matched the maneuver.

I over controlled, missed the right-hand break-down lane and dropped my right wheels onto the grassy shoulder. I came all the way off the gas not wanting to swerve too far left as I pulled back onto the interstate. The deceleration from hitting the shoulder tossed me forward against my shoulder strap. The restraint wasn't enough to keep me from bashing my face on the steering wheel. I turned my head slightly to the left and took the blow on my cheek. As I moved back onto the concrete, I could already feel my face beginning to swell. When I fully recovered and steadied the Mustang, my nemesis in the SUV was nowhere in sight.

I pulled into my parking space, stopped the engine and pulled down my sun visor. The vanity mirror on the visor confirmed my suspicions. The bruises around my right eye marked a real shiner. I knew I would take a ribbing about it and the circumstances that created the blue and purple skin around the bloodshot eye. I was right.

* * *

The rest of the week was a blur of activity. We kept our radio net and Becca busy. Each team member was assigned a specific person and the type of documents needed—trying to pin down who and how they were involved. Janet Jordan was back at work following her bout with the *flu*.

The end of each day found the whole group at my condo, where we compared notes on actions completed. Our next step was a continuation of our tasks; picking up previous threads and weaving them into our tapestry of evidence. We rotated team assignments so no one person would draw undue attention.

Each new day brought more revelations as we confirmed the flow of paperwork and payments. We also amassed photos that tied events and people to the illegal activities. Along with each image, we prepared a written narrative as corroboration.

"What are you so involved in?"

Janet Jordan's voice startled me until I realized I'd been concentrating so hard on our radio network, I must have appeared lost. "Oh, guess I finally got interested in these files I'm working on." That was lame, I thought.

"Have you been able to find out any more on Manfriedy? We haven't been out skulking around recently."

"Not really," I said. "The last couple of times I tried, I got the feeling someone was watching me. I've been cooling it lately." I also made excuses, saying that over the past weekend I got phone calls that the powers that be were satisfied nothing of major import was going on at the hospital. I said I was staying on the job because I needed the income. That apparently satisfied her; she headed back to her desk. I decided I needed to ease off on participating in the radio chatter.

I called Dennis during my lunch break on Friday and gave him a quick update on the group's work this week. He suggested that we all meet at my home on Saturday morning and told me he would coordinate with SA Williams.

41

THE SUNLIGHT WAS STREAMING THROUGH MY bedroom window Saturday morning. That was bad enough, but the primary obstacle to my sleep was a small furry puppy standing on my chest licking my face. I flipped the blanket over Sergeant York and we engaged in a faux wrestling match. This pooch was beginning to fill the void left by my old cat, PK. I relented, slid out of bed, padded to the kitchen and put food in her dish. She was torn between thanking me and the food. The food won.

Dennis and the Feeb were due soon, so I hurried through my morning rituals. The rest of the Baker Street Irregulars were also due any minute. By the time I left my bedroom, there was a tempting aroma coming from the kitchen and I knew Effie was busy out there. A cup of coffee and an orange roll was all I had time for before the doorbell rang.

By nine-thirty, the entire group assembled in my home. Before they arrived, I placed our week's efforts out on the dining table in what I hoped was a reasonable sense of order. I made sure that Special Agent Montgomery Williams knew everyone around the table. Sergeant York also made sure she introduced herself to all the folks in the room. She paused in front of each person, gave a short yip of recognition, and proceeded to the next. After a complete circuit of the table, she consigned herself to her spot in the corner of the dining room. She pawed and scratched one of her favorite blankies into a lump and settled in, keeping her eyes wide open.

I showed the evidence layout to Williams and Dennis explaining the *who, what* and *where* of each pile of documents. After thirty minutes of watching the two men pour over the files in front of them, the audience began drifting away. Even I couldn't resist the draw of a soft seat in the living room and a glass of wine. The only active eyes in the dining room apart from Dennis and Williams belonged to Sergeant York. She maintained her vigilance until her head, at last, sank down get used to *people* food onto the blanket.

Dennis and Montgomery Williams shoved back from the table and stretched. I delivered a pair of wineglasses to them and they both looked pleased. "Are you that happy to get the wine, or is our evidence good?"

"A bit of both, Casey," Dennis said.

Williams nodded in agreement. "This is a great start," he said. "I think if we round out a couple of spots, we will have enough for probable cause. That should get us warrants and we can uncover all the detail we need."

Dennis picked up a piece of paper. "We jotted down some questions we have. I think it would be a good idea to go over them with the whole group."

Effie popped her head in and said, "That sounds like something we should do right after lunch."

* * *

The only downside to one of Effie's meals is the feeling I have of needing a nap. Nevertheless, we dragged ourselves away from the kitchen and returned to the living room. I pulled a couple of dining room chairs into the room to accommodate everyone.

Dennis took the lead. "Montgomery and I think you've done a great job. We only have a couple of gaps that need filling before we go to a judge for a search order." He waved a hand to Montgomery.

"I'll echo Dennis' comments. Great job, all of you." Montgomery said. "If we can get a little more detail on how Janet Jordan handles the stolen drug sales, that will help. Also, we need a name of the person on the receiving dock who creates the "spoilage" shipments of drugs." He paused to look at notes he held. "The last item is the bank accounts. This one will be tough, but if you can identify at least one bank account number where they stash their cash, it'd be a huge step up on them." He looked at Dennis and said, "Did I miss anything?"

Dennis scanned his own notes and said, "Along with the question about bank accounts, we need to know who makes the actual deposits. Who controls the purse strings? Sidney Vickers is the overall chief of the accounting departments. Any idea whether he is part of these schemes?"

Aaron raised his hand and said, "I'm pretty sure Vickers is not involved in any of it. He's basically retired on the job, just waiting for pension day to arrive."

Dennis took the lead again. "Next topic. We need more information on the three deaths at the hospital. I don't believe in coincidences, and three is too big a number to swallow. Any ideas on what I think were murders?"

"I'm going to get second opinion autopsies," Alex said. "I have a contact who can perform an autopsy on each body. She has enough juice to contact families and get the bodies exhumed quietly. She said she would look for needle marks as a method of introducing a poison into them. She also said a total toxicology panel should be run looking for not only the usual drugs, but also for the zebras."

"What are zebras?" Aaron said.

"I guess most medical schools tell students to look for horses and not waste time looking into exotic causes—zebras," Alex said. "But in this case, we need to look at all avenues."

We delayed our examination of the crimes for supper. The group consensus settled on Chinese take-away. I put in a call to my favorite restaurant and ordered a variety of dishes—and chopsticks. I wanted to see if all these folks get cramps in their fingers handling wooden sticks as utensils like I do.

* * *

Sergeant York was still nosing around the floor under the dining table as we cleared the remnants of our Chinese meal. I don't think anyone dropped food on the floor, and the paper containers were scraped clean. That was good because I didn't want Sergeant York to get used to people food.

We stayed at the dining table to continue our discussions. "Does anyone know how you can get a person to jump off a roof of their own volition?" I said.

Dennis was the first to contribute. "The only way I can think of is suicide. They'll do it on their own. Problem is…there doesn't seem of be a suicide motive for any of these hospital employees."

"I'm sure there are drugs that can send people to their deaths. The original tox scans didn't show anything. That's why I called on the lady to do the second autopsies. She'll do a thorough job looking for horses and zebras. I also suggested she look for unusual injection sites. She told me, 'Relax Alex. I know where to look—under the tongue, between the toes, and so forth.' She almost sounded like my mother scolding me."

Ever the detective, Dennis concentrated on the deaths. "What sort of motives exist to kill these particular people?"

"Too big to be a coincidence," I said. "I can't see any motives not involving the Medicare fraud or the theft of drugs."

"Would people actually kill to cover up thefts?" Effie said.

Alex put a hand on her shoulder and said, "I'm afraid so. I've seen criminals kill for far less."

Effie shook her head, gave a heavy sigh and sank back into her chair.

With most all aspects of our activities covered, we decided to take an hour to unwind in the living room. I switched on the TV and we watched the last few minutes of some potboiler before the late news came on.

We all perked up when the newscaster referred to Little Rock General Hospital and the on-site reporter gave an update of the latest death. She reported Sam's name and the time he fell from the roof of the hospital. No mention of the two similar deaths was included.

"Can you believe it?" I said. "They're completely ignoring the fact that Sam was the third person to *fall* from the hospital roof."

"I imagine the hospital is trying to limit their liability," Montgomery Williams said. "They don't want to fuel the fire for any lawsuits."

After the news, it only took a few minutes to lay out our plans for the following week. At eleven o'clock we wrapped up our strategy session and I saw my guests out.

"Come on, Sergeant York, it's time for bed. Tomorrow, we've got a big day. I've got to coordinate the times and people to gather all the answers to questions we have." She scampered ahead of me into my bedroom.

42

ON MONDAY MORNING, I FACED THE JOURNEY TO the hospital with the same trepidation I felt that first time I began this venture, and that was nearly two months ago.

Paranoid as I am, I saw a black Chevy Suburban following me—or was it overactive imagination? I used standard tactics of speeding up, slowing down and making unnecessary turns which took me out of the way on my route to the hospital. After about ten minutes of maneuvering, I watched the SUV turn off and he was no longer on my tail.

I found a parking spot near the building—surprise. Approaching the entrance, I saw Alex shuffling along behind his sanitation cart. He put a hand to the back of his neck and moved his head as if his neck was stiff. His eyes said "meet me over here." He moved into a cross corridor leading to rest rooms and I followed.

"Did you know you a black Chevy SUV shadowed you when you entered the parking lot?" he said.

"I saw it earlier…used some defensive maneuvers and watched it turn onto a side street. I thought either I lost it or it was a coincidence."

"Can't afford to chalk anything up as a coincidence, Casey. It approached from the opposite direction as you and parked a half block down the street."

"Then he didn't follow me?"

"Nope. Trailed, as if he knew your destination. Just keep an eye out and be careful." Alex pushed his cart past me and entered the men's room.

Every team member knew their assignments for today and tomorrow. On Wednesday, each person would shift targets with the idea of throwing off any potential detection. I was surprised and pleased to learn that Janet Jordan was out with the flu—again. That afforded me more time to devote to our radio net than last week. My workload would suffer, but I figured that was a small price for the hospital to absorb in light of the money we would save them in the long run. The downside of the operation was bad publicity for them.

By shuffling file folders on a regular basis, I gave my boss, Molly Rasmussen, the appearance of a dedicated, productive worker. What I was doing was cycling folders based on time without doing any verification along the way. That gave me the opportunity to monitor and help coordinate the radio traffic.

At noon, I took my lunch break wearing my headset to maintain contact with the team. I was back at my desk and it was twelve-fifty when my earphone crackled and I heard, "Hey gang, as Archimedes said, *Eureka.*" He shouted the last word. "This is Alpha Two, I'll skip the running naked down the street, but I got it."

I heard *got what* coming from several team members.

Alex came back on the net. "Sorry not to be more specific; I found a ripped up bank deposit slip. It was in a wastebasket next to the desk of the accounts payable guy—Chet Peterson. I've seen him use a checkbook from his personal account—preprinted name info et cetera. The deposit slip I found was not from his own checkbook. I'm sure this is the one the fraud ring uses."

Subdued cheering echoed over our radio net.

"I'm going to hang around the accounting department to see if Peterson makes a trip to the bank," Alex said.

"This is a great start to the week," I said into my headset mike. "Let's see if we can cover all our weak spots in the next few days, so we don't have to regroup for another week." I signed off because I could see my boss, Molly Rasmussen looking my way.

We gathered as a group at noon on Thursday. We met for lunch in our surveillance van where we compared notes from our week's activities. I went over the punch-list I put together after the last meeting with the police and FBI. I read each entry from the list, and the name of the person who was to gather the evidence. In turn, as the parties indicated affirmative outcomes, I ticked the item off the list. When we finished out meeting, there were only three matters remaining on our To Do list.

We made detailed plans to complete the last of our chores on Friday. After that, the topic turned to my black eye, which was only beginning to fade, and how I got it.

Falcon seemed the most concerned. "I think we need to find out who belongs to that black Chevy Suburban. Could be part of the fraud and thefts we're looking into. And if it is, they could help us tie details together. If it doesn't, well, we still need to know. Can anyone think of a reason?"

No one spoke up. I said, "I can't think of anyone or any reason."

Falcon turned to me. "You've been involved in a couple of situations recently. Could it be spillover from either of those?"

Situations? If you call murder situations. "I can't think of anything…which leaves us with…what?"

"Which leaves us with somebody from this current investigation," Falcon said. "And, if we can't ID these people, we could be in a world of hurt."

43

ON THE WAY HOME, I SPOTTED MY *FRIENDS* IN THE big ol' Chevy. I decided to give them a workout. A couple of turns confirmed my suspicions—they were tailing me. I pulled into a familiar strip mall. I know a boutique there which has a side door away from the main entrance. I parked on the side street and walked back to the front entrance. Inside, I browsed, keeping an eye on their SUV parked near the main door.

I knew if I waited long enough, they would wonder if I slipped out. After fifteen minutes, my ploy worked. I saw the passenger ease out of the vehicle and start toward the storefront. Between the hood he wore pulled up and my efforts to stay between clothes racks, I wasn't able to see him well enough for an ID.

When he neared the entrance, I moved through the side door and hurried to my Mustang. I drove around the block and came along the row of parked cars where the Chevy Suburban idled next to the curb. The tinted windows prevented me from seeing the driver plainly—all I could say was, large, male.

The SUV driver saw my car and laid on his horn. His partner spun around, hustled back to the Chevy and leapt into the passenger seat. By that time I was rounding a corner and soon was out of their sight.

At home, I detailed the events of my drive home to Aaron and Effie. "Are you sure it's a good idea to antagonize those people?" Effie asked.

"I'm tired of being on the short end of the stick—the end with all the dung on it. In the inimitable words of Buford T. Justice, the sheriff in the 'Smokey and the Bandit' movie when he said. 'I gonna be the pursuor and they gonna be da pursuees' or somethin' like that."

I managed to elicit a smile from Effie, however Aaron's brow remained furrowed. "C'mon, Aaron. It's been a good week," I said. "Can't we relax a bit?"

He shrugged. "I suppose…but we still have a big hole at the pinnacle of our family crime tree."

He was right. We were confident we knew the players in the Medicare fraud and the drug thefts; we knew the routing number of the bank account they used to run the money in and out. But…we all felt there was a missing link at the top. The person who controlled and coordinated the entire scheme. We tossed around the names of everybody we knew to be involved and some on the periphery who *might* be part of the plot.

"Well, we've still got a big chore left for tomorrow," I said. I got up and started clearing our dinner dishes.

Aaron gathered some of the dirty plates. "Should we put a single person on each suspect and try to smoke them out?"

Effie loaded the dishes into the dishwasher. "We have too many suspects. The group won't stretch that far."

I nodded. "You're right. Best thing we can all do is float and cover as much ground as possible looking for leads." I waited for objections—there were none. "I'll circulate the word to the rest of our gang."

I had a strange feeling as I started for bed after the evening news. Nothing I could put a finger on, but that old tingle was running up and down my spine. I didn't sleep well.

44

I FELT OPTIMISTIC FRIDAY MORNING WHEN I OPENED the drapes in my room to a bright clear, day. Felt good until… the phone rang.

It was Alex and he was setting up a conference call with our entire group. Effie, Aaron and I crowded around my cell with the speaker function turned on.

Alex did a quick head count to be sure everyone was on the line before he started. "I got a preliminary autopsy report."

"What did your M.E. say? What did she find?" I said.

"My M.E., actually she's a forensic pathologist, found a toxin in the first body, Gloria Sexton."

A chorus of "Why only one?" interrupted him. He told the group that Sam Atkinson's body wasn't available yet and he'd explain why nothing was found in Roberta Blackwood's body.

Alex picked up the narrative again. "She found a drug called scopolamine. It's odorless and tasteless. It's like the date rape drug, Rohypnol, on steroids. Depending on the dosage, it can cause anything from mild euphoria…to depleting your entire bank account…to killing yourself—"

"Alex, this is Falcon…excuse the interruption. How did she find anything after embalming?"

"The Coroner's Office took blood, urine and hair samples at the time of the original autopsy. Fortunately, those samples were preserved and available for our second examination."

"What did the samples tell her about the deaths?" I said.

Before Alex could answer my question, Falcon added another. "Was it injected with a needle?"

"Hang on," Alex said. "I'll get to everything in due course."

I thought I caught a hint of exasperation in his tone. I heard Alex take a deep breath before he continued. "The doc said that an injection was one way to introduce it, and she's had plenty of experience checking drug users. She also said it would be difficult to ask someone to strip down 'because I want to inject you where the sun don't shine.' Since it doesn't have any taste, it's more likely the drug was administered in liquid form...as in a soda—could have been in anything."

I could hear several of the group breathing on the phone line.

Alex picked up his narrative again. "Our doc found the scopolamine in the hair sample from Sexton. Her theory is that the killer was unsure of the dosage needed and experimented on Sexton. She believes that because it can take a few days for the drug to show up in a hair sample, they tried different doses over a matter of days on Sexton. They figured out how much was needed and gave Blackwood the necessary dose the first time out. Because of that, her hair sample was clean. And...Sam Atkinson's body or hair samples weren't available to her when she began her examinations. By inference however, she is confident that the second death was a homicide as well. Atkinson's cause of death will need further investigation, but the way he died—the MO of his death—leads to the homicide conclusion as well. Any more questions?"

Everyone on the line was silent.

"Since introduction of the drug was most likely in a liquid laced with scopolamine, everyone should exercise caution. Beware of Greeks bearing gifts," Alex said.

We all muttered agreement, and I signed off the conference call.

Even with all that, I still felt upbeat. One of the main reasons was the great breakfast Effie and Aaron prepared. We were closing in on the last of the evidence gathering phase with a couple of weeks to spare on our self-imposed deadline.

Effie decided to ride to the hospital with me and we enjoyed the sunshine beating down on us with the Mustang's top stored in it receptacle behind the rear seats. I dropped Effie on the far side of the hospital, away from the parking lot. That would give us separation as we entered.

In my office, I grabbed a pile of folders to check, settled in at my desk and plugged the Bluetooth phone device into my ear. I listened to the chatter on the radio and plowed through a good stack of work. I even skipped my morning break to listen to the activity.

I wasn't hearing much in the way of positive news. It seemed like every prospective perp, including my co-worker, Janet Jordan, and my boss, Molly Rasmussen, was on the move around the building. I could hear the frustration in the voices of our group, doing their best to update everyone and to keep up with their assigned quarry. Even Harriet Manfriedy, the head of HR, was adding to the chaos.

Becca had told me about the hospital schematic she devised and covered with plastic so she could use erasable dry markers on it. I sensed her frustration level rising and pictured her scribbling on the map, erasing people and routes trying to make sense of the confusion.

I began to wonder if the bad guys were on to us and this was their deliberate effort to thwart our surveillance. I found myself dwelling on that thought to the point depression was settling in on me. I shook my head to clear the cobwebs and spoke loud enough the headset mike could pick it up. "Hey, gang. Let's take a break. Slow down, grab some lunch and let's restart the effort around one o'clock."

Grunts of agreement echoed around our network. I grabbed my purse and made my way to the cafeteria.

"Mind if I join you?"

I looked up and saw Janet approaching my table. "No, grab a chair and park it." Without looking up, I said, "I'm feeling lonely in the office today. You and Molly have been on the run since early this morning. Anything special going on?"

Waiting for an answer was agonizing. I held my breath to drag it out. I was beginning to think I would have to rush into the vacuum of silence. Just as I decided to break the hush myself, Janet said, "I don't guess there's anything special. Me, I had a lot of personal business I needed to attend to. Don't know what Molly was doing."

I left the subject alone and went back to my meal without adding anything. Not much of an investigation on my part. I was wondering if anyone on the team would be doing any better.

The rest of the afternoon was as dismal as the morning session. By the time I left for home, the weather turned to match the day I was experiencing. Unlike this morning when we enjoyed the wind blowing in on us, I drove with the top and windows up; the wipers going full blast. The metronome action and sound of the windshield wipers going swish-swish added to the dreariness of the day. I did my best to raise my spirits by looking forward to our group meeting, but it was a waste of time.

* * *

At home, Effie was her usual cheery self as she bustled around. "Cheer up, Casey. Things could be worse."

"How?" I said, and with a shrug left the question hanging in the air.

45

THE MOOD OF OUR GROUP WAS NO BETTER THAN mine. After admitting nothing was accomplished today, we brainstormed for new ideas. The process was going well, when my cell rang.

It was Dennis and I put him on speaker. "We've come up with a new idea for the evidence gathering." He paused, and I suspect it was simply for affect. Then he said, "We believe we need fingerprints of all the suspects. Shouldn't be hard."

"Are you out of your gourd?" I asked. "We've been busting our butts for you and now at this late date you want fingerprints." I hoped my exasperation showed through in my voice. "And who is the 'we' you refer to?"

There was a long pause before Dennis said, "Well, the FBI came up with the request."

"I might have known. The Feeb sits back, feet up on his desk no doubt, and wants to play field-general."

"That's not fair, Casey and you know it," Dennis said.

"I know. I'm just frustrated. Of course, we'll see what we can do."

That news set off a flurry of conversation. We swapped brainstorming subjects and worked on how and where we might find the needed fingerprints.

Around three p.m., Falcon reached into a pocket, checked the screen on his phone and left the table. I only caught a few words: "when? where?…okay, meet you at your work tomorrow about noon."

It was nearly six o'clock by the time we wrapped up our session. I was moving toward the front door when Falcon took me aside. "I've got some business tomorrow around noon. How about coming with me and I'll buy you lunch."

I hesitated.

Falcon took me by the arm. "I know it's been a rough week. Come along tomorrow and I'll get your mind off this business." He waved his arm in a half circle toward the dining table.

This time I nodded, wondering what business he needed to take care of on a weekend.

* * *

Knowing Falcon's habits, I was in place in front of my condo building at a quarter to twelve. He picked me up at eleven fifty-five. The route he took was familiar, and I wasn't surprised when he parked in front of Augustino's restaurant. "What business do you have to conduct here?"

"Remember our waiter the night we ate here?" I nodded and he continued. "When I followed him to the kitchen, he told me a story and I said I'd lend a hand. Won't take long and then we can eat."

When we were seated, Falcon excused himself and I saw he was conversing with Paddy near the kitchen. Too far away to hear anything. Falcon returned and sat down. I waited for him to explain. "Sometimes it's like pulling teeth to get anything out of you." I let out a long sigh and stared at him. I vowed to myself I would not say another word until he spoke.

A waiter, not the one Falcon spoke to, brought our drinks. Falcon looked up and said, "Paddy is having a spot of trouble with some folks he borrowed money from."

"Loan shark?"

"Yep. He has the money ready to pay off the loan, but now this guy is stalling and trying to tack more onto the vig. I told him I'd get the shark out of the picture."

I let the story drop there and went back to my sandwich. As we were finishing lunch, Falcon said, "Need to wait for a call, but come with me this afternoon and you can see me at work."

Figuring that might be fun, I invited Falcon to my condo. "That way, when you get a call we can leave from there."

* * *

Falcon arrived and since he was a bit early, Effie and Aaron joined us to talk about the coming week's efforts. We were still looking for ways to gather fingerprints.

The best would be on drinking glasses, but those were in scarce supply around the hospital offices. Coffee cups would be good, yet they had the same downside as glasses. Too many paper cups in use, and if a person had a ceramic coffee mug, it would soon be missed. The consensus seemed to be soft drink cans.

Effie disappeared into the kitchen and we soon heard her call of "soup's on." She laughed as she came back into the dining room carrying a tray of sandwiches. "No soup today," she said.

Falcon and I begged off on the lunch, since we already ate before coming home. A little after one o'clock, Falcon answered his cell. His conversation was short with only a couple of words from him. He looked at me and said, "We're on for two-fifteen in the parking lot of the restaurant."

"On for what?" Effie asked.

Since I didn't tell either Aaron or Effie of the help Falcon was providing to the waiter at Augustino's, she was in the dark. "This doesn't have anything to do with our project." I said. "Just a little extra curricular side play. We shouldn't be gone very long."

46

FALCON DROVE TO THE RESTAURANT IN SILENCE. I wondered if he was preparing a plan or rehearsing it in his mind. At last he glanced my direction. "Do you have your Glock with you?"

"I'm not sure why I brought it along, but yes, it's in my purse."

"Okay, then. When we get to the parking lot, you can come with me to meet this guy—Paddy called him Duke. I ran a background on him and his actual name is Alberto Vincenzo. I want you to stay behind me, between me and the car. If the deal goes sideways, make for the car and get the hell outta Dodge. Use your gun *only* as a last resort."

The dash clock in Falcon's car read one-thirty when he pulled into a parking spot and put the car in Park. He handed me the keys and said "Remember what I told you. No heroics." He was out of the car and walking toward the back entrance to the restaurant.

I stumbled out of the car door and followed him. We waited…

Around two-twenty, a large black Cadillac sedan slid into the lot. As soon as the car stopped, a large man exited the vehicle and started toward the restaurant's back door. When he was fifteen feet from us, Falcon said, "Eh! I'm the guy you're looking for."

"Don't think so," he said. "I'm after a runty Mick who waits tables here."

"That's rather unkind language, isn't it?" Falcon moved two paces closer to the larger man. "What's your name?"

"Duke. What's it to you?"

"Just wanted to be sure I was going to send the right person packing, Alberto."

Duke didn't seem amused. Using his real name seemed to upset him. He said, "Get the hell outta my way or I'll—"

"Keep talking like that and you'll be spitting teeth all over the asphalt. I have your last payment from Paddy, less that last hundred you tacked onto the vig…and minus another hundred for my trouble."

"You talk mighty big, fellow. Are you packing?"

Falcon opened his jacket and pulled it up, then turned a full circle in place. "You can see I'm not armed. I don't think I'll need a weapon to settle this."

The two men stepped forward until they were arm's length apart. Falcon set his feet and I could see his right hand down at his side. He curled the fingers into a fist and extended the thumb over the top so it jutted beyond the fist. Duke telegraphed a roundhouse right and Falcon stepped inside the arc of the swing and drove his right thumb into the man's solar plexus. I heard a whoosh as Duke expelled a gush of air. Duke regained his balance and charged forward. Falcon sidestepped to the left and drove that thumb into the Duke's right kidney area.

Falcon swung around and followed behind Duke's body ramming the thumb into the other kidney. Falcon did a tattoo of thumb jabs up the man's spine. Duke hung in the air until Falcon kicked the back of the left knee, then Duke crumpled to the concrete.

With one clean swipe, Falcon jerked the man's gun from the small of his back. He dropped the magazine from the pistol's butt, yanked the slide to the rear and stripped it from the grip and trigger. Falcon tossed the three pieces of the weapon in different directions. He bent down, and in a low growl said, "Alberto, here's your money as I explained earlier. Your business with Paddy is finished and he doesn't owe anything more. If I hear you've come back…and I *will* hear…we'll go for a second round. You will not like the results. You can walk away from this one…you won't be able to walk after the next round. Do you understand me?"

Duke grunted but nothing was distinguishable. Falcon said, "Do you understand?"

Duke muttered a *yeah*.

"Good," Falcon said. "Casey, let's get out of here. I feel like a beer."

My eyebrows shot up my forehead and my mouth gaped open. I was in awe of what I just witnessed. I did my best to say something, but nothing came. I simply followed Falcon back to his car.

47

WE GATHERED AT MY HOME FOR THE AFTERNOON. Becca and Alex joined the group. Aaron said, "What were you and Falcon up to this afternoon?"

"You should have seen it. Don't ever mess with his thumb," I said. Then I looked at Falcon for a signal that would tell me if it was okay to tell the bunch what happened in the parking lot. All I got from him was a raised eyebrow shrug. I took that as a go-ahead, so I regaled the team with the details of this afternoon's events.

After the ooh's and ah's subsided, the talk moved on to the gathering of fingerprints from our suspects. It appeared to be an impossible challenge. No one seemed to have an easy answer.

Sergeant York made her usual rounds and, satisfied no one in the crowd posed an imminent danger, she settled onto her bed in the corner of the room. Most of the rest of us grabbed a seat in the living room after filling a mug with steaming coffee. A quiet settled over the group like a *cone of silence* from the old TV show with only a low hum of voices from the television.

* * *

Aaron and Effie prepared a buffet style supper of cold cuts, breads, salad items, and bottles of salad dressing for the evening meal. Everyone retired to the dining room table with plates heaped high with more than enough to eat.

As usual, the conversation returned to our tasks at the hospital. I wheeled out the big white board and started putting notes on it.

We congratulated ourselves on our accomplishments and bemoaned those tasks which were still unfulfilled. On an unrelated item, we talked about the two men and the Chevy SUV.

We still had no idea who they were and what they wanted or needed. Guesses were flying around the table.

"The only two people who come close to the descriptions are the U.S. Marshalls guarding Janet Jordan," said Alex. "How could they be involved?"

The question hung in the air with no answer coming.

Falcon said he would look into these men and asked Alex if he would lend a hand.

"I've got a few friends back in D.C. who might shed some light on them," Alex said.

Our talk turned to the extras the authorities needed. We had a few ideas about obtaining fingerprints, but they also wanted more detail on the bank transactions. Beyond that, Dennis told us what they expected the bad guys were going to try. They had a date in mind and expected to close down their operations and head for countries with nonexistent extradition laws.

We were told the cops and the FBI would be really happy if we could pin down the exact date of the wrap up. They would also like any email communications between the conspirators, plus details and exact amounts of money siphoned off and deposited to their own accounts.

Well…I guess we would be happy to get that information too…but our discussions didn't bring up much in the way we could accomplish those goals. Several ideas bounced around the table, but none bore fruit

I smacked my forehead. "CrackerJack." I surprised myself at how loud I shouted the name.

"I'll have some popcorn," said Aaron.

Effie leapt to her feet. "I remember him."

"Go ahead, Effie. Tell the group," I said.

"Okay." Effie looked around to see if everyone was paying attention. "CrackerJack is a talented computer hacker. He helped us when Casey was working at Cyber-Technology. Really helped us solve the murders there."

Now, it was my turn again. "I met him before that, but he was a help solving those crimes at Cyber-Technology. I met with him after that, and I got the impression he was working on a federal job. He wouldn't tell who, but when I ran through a litany of three-letter acronyms; he flinched when I mentioned the NSA. He held out and wouldn't say anymore."

Alex interrupted. "It might have well been the National Security Agency. Every year they scour the country for bright computer people. When NSA finds someone who fits their bill, they hire the person on a temporary basis."

"What do they hire them for?" Aaron said.

"The NSA tosses them problems which have been stumping their own analysts. With a fresh eye and perspective, these temps often solve problems plaguing the agency. Obviously, each temp they hire signs a secrecy agreement. That's why this CrackerJack played it cagey when you questioned him, Casey."

I put in a call to CrackerJack and got an electronic mailbox. I told him I could use his help and reminded him of my phone numbers. A total waste of time; I knew CrackerJack automated his operation to the hilt and no doubt had me cross-referenced several ways.

I had no idea how long it would take CrackerJack to return my call. From past experience, I knew he could dive into the electronics working on a problem and not surface for days. I suggested we go back to the white board.

We haggled over our problems the rest of the evening. I filled the white board and was forced to turn it over and start on the second side. A lot of writing and few solutions. We all seemed dragged out and drained.

I suggested we take a break and watch the late evening news on TV. I gave up on a return call from CrackerJack. The news was over and the late-night talk shows were on. I started to flip through the networks, but the phone rang. I muted the television and raced for the phone. The caller ID appeared on the TV screen, but gave no information: Out of Area, Out of Area; which is shorthand for No name; no phone number.

I nearly broke my neck getting to the phone. I was right; CrackerJack was returning my call. I punched the speaker button and said, "How you doing? Do you mind if I have you on speakerphone?"

CrackerJack said, "You don't have any members of law enforcement in the audience, do you?"

"I'm officially a CI, it that counts."

There was a clattering of a keyboard in the background. "That don't count, Casey. I trust you."

I outlined the cases we were working on and the type of information we needed. There was a long pause before CrackerJack came back on the line. "Okay, babe. I'll need more detail, but I gotta tell you I'm up to my ass in alligators. It's gonna be at least two weeks before I can get to it."

"We haven't got two weeks," I said.

"I got three on my plate ahead of you. You got any play in your deadline?"

When I told him we were up against a one-week drop-dead date he said, "Okay, I'll need background on where the crimes are occurring..." Keyboard clatter filled the pause again. "... you know, the names, first and last and middle if you got it... for everyone—any detail you got on bank accounts—and...any other facts you think are important. I'll get back to you when I can. That's the best I can do, Casey."

I promised to get all the information I had to him in an email tonight. I could see a short night's sleep coming.

48

NO WONDER I FELT CRAPPY WHEN I GOT UP THIS morning. I was up until three a.m. preparing the email to CrackerJack. After that, I did my whirling dervish imitation for another hour. Now I was facing a new week at the hospital with a self-imposed deadline of two to three weeks from now. My day got a lot brighter when I reached the kitchen to find Aaron and Effie racing about in aprons.

Thirty minutes at the kitchen table and two cups of coffee put me in a cheerful mood. I actually whistled while I showered, at least as close to whistling as I can manage.

The weather said "top down" and I listened to Mother Nature. The wind racing over and around the windshield bolstered my spirits. By the time I walked into the hospital, I was on top of the hill. Shortly the saying: beware the moral high ground, because it's downhill in all directions—began nagging at me.

I listened to our radio net all morning as I shuffled folders on my desktop. Alex moved around looking for the fraud folders being passed from one suspect to another. Each time he got close, his quarry disappeared. Effie was sniffing around Human Resources—doing her best to follow the scent of Harriet Manfriedy. The lady did leave a trail of odor in her wake. Again, our efforts were thwarted. Somehow, Harriet ditched the article of clothing that was reeking of her overpowering perfume.

Aaron checked in with yet another disappointment. He was to look for bank account numbers and transactions but found none. It was like there was nothing out of the ordinary. I was beginning to think the crooks were wise to us and were leading us around by the nose. I suggested each member of the team swap tasks and try again. An hour of that tack still produced no gains.

I mentally pulled another chunk of hair out of my head, stacked my work into a single pile, and headed for the cafeteria. I was certain if I fortified my body with something high in the two major food groups—starch and fat—I would be able to put a stop to our failures and set us back on track. I don't think it worked because I heard a couple of arteries snap shut and no epiphanies.

I dialed CrackerJack on my cell phone and got the expected response. I didn't bother leaving a message; if interested, he would read my number in his caller ID.

The afternoon was a repeat of the morning. By three p.m. our group decided to call off any more efforts at gathering evidence. Instead, we agreed to meet at my condo to assess our efforts.

The evening passed in silence except for a couple of outbursts that led to nothing. I didn't bother dragging out the white board. I buried my nose in the newspapers and gazed at the television screen with a blank stare.

* * *

A second day of disappointment followed. I began to wonder if our entire impetus was dissipated. Call after call on our radio net reported dead-ends, lost opportunities and near misses.

I labored through the day hoping against hope there would be a ray of sunshine somewhere in the middle of our floundering. No such luck. At five o'clock, I piled my work folders on the corner of my desk and slipped on my jacket. Janet Jordan looked at me and said, "Casey, you look like you lost your best friend. Anything I can do to help?"

I swore there was a look on her face saying "we foiled you again, didn't we?" I forced a smile. "No, nothing. I'm a bit down over things outside of work." I'm getting better at lying.

Yesterday's sunshine turned dark and showers swept the roads. I hunched over the Mustang's steering wheel and listened to the sound of the wiper blades. It was a hypnotic two-note metronome: swish – swoosh; swish – swoosh. I needed to shake my head to clear the cobwebs and concentrate on the highway. *Perhaps the bad weather will bring better luck at finding evidence.* So much for that theory. The end of the day brought little in the way of results.

Becca stopped by my condo and we ate dinner with Effie and Aaron. Their moods were down on my level. Small talk filled the void as we avoided the evidence gathering that was flagging. I invited Becca to spend the night, but she opted to go home to a familiar bed.

My roomies and I did get to the job at hand, but we didn't get much past an updated list of items we still needed to collect… and no way of gathering the needed evidence. Aaron and Effie excused themselves and headed to bed around ten-fifteen. I stared at the television screen—lost in empty thoughts. I have no idea what the late-night comedians said. At midnight, I gave up and went to bed. I fell asleep with little effort.

The ringing phone on my nightstand jarred me awake. I jerked upright and looked at the clock. It was three forty-four in the morning. I reached for the phone fearing the worst and said, "Who the hell is calling at this hour?"

49

I MUTTERED TO MYSELF AND FORCED MY EYES OPEN enough to locate my phone. As I picked it up, I heard, "Hey, babe. How you doing?"

"CrackerJack, is that you? Do you know what time it is?"

"I dunno. Late I guess."

"Late? It's about three-thirty in the morning. What are you doing up at this hour?"

CrackerJack said, "I took a look at your stuff and decided to go online to see what I could see. It's real interesting and I put you on the front burner. I got a good start on the answers and I can give you most of what you want by tomorrow evening."

"CrackerJack, what's tomorrow to you?"

"I dunno. What day is this?"

"It's almost four a.m. on Wednesday. So, when do you think you'll have something?"

"Better make it late Thursday. Okay? I'm back to it."

I started to say good-bye, but I was already talking to a dead phone connection. I rolled over with the biggest grin on my face, did a bicycle peddling motion with my feet in the air, and added a couple of fist pumps just for good measure. Sergeant York stood on the far corner of the bed, as far from me as she could get without falling off. She hunched her shoulders, cocked her head and stared at me. "It's okay, girl. Good news makes me do that."

Knowing I would never get back to sleep, I sat up on the side of my bed. I slid my feet into my slippers and grabbed for my robe. My plan was to spread the good news to Aaron and Effie. Sergeant York decided she should accompany me.

My eyes fell on my bedside clock and saw the digital numbers—4-4-4. Maybe I should give my roommates another two hours of sleep.

* * *

I forced myself to stay in bed for another forty-five minutes before I made my way to the kitchen. Boiling water and coffee I can handle, and I hoped the aroma would bring at least one of my roomies out to share a cup with me. I was bursting to tell someone CrackerJack was on the job.

The morning paper was outside the condo door. I banged around and slammed the front door. No reaction from anyone. I called to Sergeant York. She headed toward me from an unknown location, her toenails clattered on bare floor as she rounded the corner into the kitchen. I did my best melodramatic overacting routine getting food for my pooch.

I was putting a food dish down on the floor when Aaron stumbled into the room. "Alright, all ready. You've made enough noise to wake everyone in the building. Do I recognize a pattern here?"

"You bet. I've got some great news from CrackerJack."

"He's cracked the entire case!"

"Well, no but he's interested and put us at the top of his list. He should have details for us tomorrow night."

I felt like I was floating on clouds. I looked out my front window and yesterday's bad weather was still with us. Even with the gloomy clouds, I was still on top of the world and expecting to gather in a batch of evidence today. When Effie came into the kitchen, it gave me the opportunity to relate my good news again. I grabbed my phone and told the rest of our crew about CrackerJack and we coordinated ideas for the day ahead.

When I arrived at work, Molly wasn't at her desk. Janet Jordan came in right after me. We used the time for gossip and sipping coffee. Janet sat down at her desk and put her back to me. That made it easy for me to slip on my radio network headset.

I listened to our crew sort out positions and ease into a routine moving around and looking for evidence. Our boss came into the office and I shuffled folders on my desk. That always satisfied Molly and she didn't care whether I accomplished anything. Looking at Janet's back, it seemed to me she applied the same sham to her workload.

By nine-thirty I was ready for a break. I was tired of listening to the radio net. Our group wasn't getting anything done either. Once again, the team was running in circles. Janet and I took our morning break together in the cafeteria. On our way back to the office, I plugged my radio earpiece in again and pretended to make a cell phone call. The first thing I heard was: Tora, Tora. I couldn't believe what I heard. It was an agreed upon warning the net was compromised. The only reason someone would use these words, meant one of our radios was in the hands of someone outside our group. I couldn't be sure who gave the warning signal. It was a male voice, but I still wasn't sure.

Our emergency procedures also included a backup plan following the emergency words. We all switched to a secondary frequency, and only someone who had pertinent information was to speak. After that, we were to go silent and regroup after work. I managed to change frequencies on my radio just in time to hear Aaron, "This is Alpha One; Echo and Foxtrot are in trouble."

For a day that began so bright, the crap sure hit the fan. I was wondering how I would be able to last until the end of the day.

* * *

The second hand on the office wall clock would make a glacier look like the turtle in the hare and tortoise story. I stretched my afternoon break as long as I could. Here, I could watch people rather than the clock. Molly was gone from the office by the time I returned.

As I sat down, Janet pushed back from her desk and spun her chair around to face me. "How was your break?" I didn't respond and she pushed her way into the silence. "Well, how is your investigation going?"

I was sure Janet was going to press the issue until I responded. "There's not much to say about the investigation. I pretty much hit a dead end and the authorities told me to cool it."

"That's too bad. I was enjoying the chase as long as no one was chasing me."

The grin on her face said "joke," so I chuckled as in my best fake laugh. "Do you think there are any leads we could follow?"

"I think there may be something happening in Human Resources. I don't trust the head of the place, Harriet Manfriedy. She's up to no good; I'd bet a bunch on it."

I looked at her for a full minute thinking she would add information on her own. When she held her silence as long as I did, I knew she had interview and interrogation practice. "If you have details, Janet, I think you should share it with me. I thought we had a sister-ship going here." This time, I was determined to keep the pressure on her until she caved. I didn't have to wait as long as I expected.

"I do feel close to you, Casey, but I'm conflicted. Let me think about it overnight, and I'll let you know tomorrow."

I nodded and we both went back to our stacks of folders. I couldn't help wondering if she knew something…and if she would actually confide in me. The second hand resumed its inchworm crawl around the dial.

I couldn't believe my eyes. I got so caught up in the file folders on my desk, I lost track of time. When I looked up, it was five minutes till quitting time. I stacked my folders, gathered my purse and headed for the door. "See you in the morning, Janet," I said over my shoulder without looking back.

I made it to the parking lot at a dog trot and headed toward the van. All four flashers on the surveillance van blinked two times. What the hell else could be wrong?

I veered off the course to the van and looked for my own car. My head was spinning. First Effie and Falcon were in some kind of trouble and now Becca was signaling it was not safe to approach the van. Now what? Might as well head for home and hope everyone would check in.

50

I OPENED THE DOOR TO MY HOME AND STEPPED IN. I thought I saw something out of the corner of my eye and glanced toward the top shelf of the coat tree to my right. I expected to see PK perched up there in his vulture pose. "Damn, PK. I do miss you." I squinted my eyes to force the tears back.

Effie was already home, and she described her afternoon. Hospital security grabbed her and was going to hand her over to the Little Rock police. She said, "Do you remember the self-defense course we took?"

I nodded, but she was already going into the rest of the story. "It's amazing. Even these sneakers did the job. I used my foot to stomp on the top of his instep. The security guy was still howling when I went through the door. I don't think he even came after me because I didn't see anyone all the way to the bus stop."

"Did you hear anything from Falcon?"

"He called here just after I got home. He's okay, but his cover is blown. We were lucky. Nobody who saw him when he rescued Becca from the hospital cops was around. All they know is he was using a false hospital ID."

"How about you?"

"They confiscated my ID badge before I took off—grabbed my radio too. I forgot to tell you they have Falcon's radio as well."

I shook my head. "That pretty well shoots our communications network."

Looking down, Sergeant York was making circle-eights around my legs. "I swear, dog, I think you've got some cat in you. Hungry? Food?" One of those words registered; the circling stopped, to be followed by short hops in the air. The hops continued until I got her food dish and filled it. The hops stopped and she assumed a crouched position in front of her dish and then wolfed it down.

We set up a conference call with the group. Falcon confirmed the hospital goons confiscated his ID card and radio before letting him go. Becca told us she spotted someone with binoculars watching the van. That's why she used the flasher lights warning signal. No one approached her, so she left and drove out of the lot. She was still on the streets making certain she wasn't being followed. "It's gonna be thirty to forty minutes before I can get to your place, Casey. I'm darn near out to the airport by now," she said.

The whole group at the condo pitched in and set up a buffet supper. The missing members straggled in, and Alex was the last to arrive. He dropped a medium size sports bag in the corner of the dining room. I was surprised how comfortable everyone was in the kitchen—except me. I am still the queen of boiled water, but beyond that I'm a basic klutz. The pressure of the day was giving me a headache. I found a bottle of Tylenol in a kitchen cabinet and shook two tablets into my hand. I retrieved a glass from the same cabinet and filled it from the dispenser in the refrigerator door. I popped the pills into my mouth, took a swig of water and tossed my head back to swallow them.

I noticed Effie looking at me. "What?" I said.

She gave me an apprehensive look before she said anything. "There is a better way to make sure pills go down the right way…a nurse told me about it." Effie waited a beat to see if I said anything. I didn't and she continued. "Put a pill in your mouth; take a drink of water and tilt you head down—not up. That way the pill is almost guaranteed to be swallowed the correct way."

I stared at her and said, "Girl, you never cease to amaze me. How do you accumulate so much information?"

"I read and listen a lot."

Aaron said, "Soup's on."

* * *

Everybody agreed and the entire mealtime was filled with trivial, mindless banter. My headache was in remission and I realized how much I needed some down time. I was getting stale with no new ideas for our problems.

Forty-five minutes gave us all time to eat and rejuvenate our minds. Alex brought us out of our reverie and back to the problem at hand. He said, "Where do we stand on the evidence we need for the authorities?"

"Not all that good," I said. "I'd say we're about seventy percent there."

"That doesn't sound all that bad," Aaron said.

"Most of the hard evidence, that is the paperwork, is about complete," I said. "Only hope that CrackerJack can come through with enough electronic intel to tie all the people we suspect to the crimes."

Alex told us it would take him several days to come up with enough equipment to replace our entire compromised communications network. He retrieved the sports bag from the corner and said, "These will serve as a stopgap." As he walked around the table, he gave each of us two boxes. "They're prepaid cell phones, each with a small Bluetooth earbud."

Falcon stood and said, "Hope you didn't use a credit card to buy them."

Alex stopped and looked at Falcon. "Of course not—cash only. And I didn't buy more than two at any one location. Shouldn't be any problems anyone will be able to track us down through the phones." He pulled one out of the box and held it up. "I marked each with our phonetic IDs." Displaying his phone an A2 was visible on it. "I also took time to program each phone with all our numbers in the speed dial system."

"My apologies. Looks like you've been busy on your way here," Falcon said.

Our discussion then focused on how we could gather anything more with a limited crew and limited-to-no communications. We would be forced to operate independently and in the dark as to what the rest of the members of the group were doing. We decided that Becca could still monitor the general situation from the van and we could use the cell phones Alex bought to talk with one another.

Since we would not have two-way communications with all the group, we set up a work-around. When someone had info for one person, they would call that person's phone and that would end the comms. If the information was for everyone, we would dial one of the team and relay the message and with a pass-it-on tag. The information could then be relayed from person-to-person in alphabetical order.

My cell rang and I saw by the caller ID it was CrackerJack. I told him I was putting him on speaker and ran down the people in the room. "We're going to need you even more than before," I said.

"Okay, babe. Just called to say it's going good. Got a lot. Just not organized yet. I'll have it tomorrow night. See ya."

The connection was gone. Everyone around the table was looking at the phone with the same puzzled expression on their face. Aaron said it for all of us, "There's a young man in a hurry."

51

THE NEXT MORNING, I WAS READY TO LEAVE FOR work when Sergeant York came around the corner into the hall with a clickity-click. "You need your nails clipped," I said. The Yorkie-poo slid to a stop, sat down and stared at me. When I took a step toward her, she backed up matching me step for step. "Darned if you don't know what I'm saying. C'mon, I know you don't like your nails clipped. Give me a kiss." The words were no more out of my mouth when Sergeant York ran toward me and jumped into my arms. I scratched her back, kissed her on the head and put her down. "See you later," I said. She trotted back into the living room and headed for one of several of her sleeping pads.

At the office my workload didn't improve or keep me busy. Janet divided her time between shuffling the files on her desk and looking at me. I asked her to go with me on our morning break. The look on her face said she was happy to spend time with me.

I was again mulling over whether I could trust Janet or not. She seemed to have a reserved aspect, and I wondered what that side hid. On our morning break, Janet was so effervescent, I wasn't sure I could get an accurate read. For someone in the Witness Protection Program, she didn't seem to have a care in the world. Again, she asked if she could become more active in the hunt for our local bad guys.

"There have been so many close calls, I decided to put the whole affair on the back burner," I said.

Janet cocked her head and said, "Close calls? What do you mean?"

I didn't want to divulge details, and felt like I'd backed myself into a corner. *This is going to take some fast thinking and fancy footwork.* "Hmm," was the only sound coming out of my mouth. *So much for fast thinking.* I took a swig of my coffee and wiped my mouth with a napkin—stalling for time. "It's so far on the back burner, I don't even want to talk about it."

Every time I made any kind of move, Janet was at my elbow. Try as I might, I could not ditch her. In desperation, I headed for the restroom. When I entered, she held back and I got into a stall as quick as I could. Grabbing my special cell phone, I dialed Aaron and since I wasn't sure if she followed me in here I whispered a message. "Aaron, Janet is stuck to me like a leech; I won't be able to do anything today. Tell the rest to do what they can; pass it on."

I stood up and prepared to leave. This was a false visit and I almost forgot to flush the toilet. When I opened the stall door, there she was. "Janet, I didn't think I needed help taking a pee."

"Just wanted to repair my makeup. Ready for a cafeteria break?"

On the inside I cringed, but said, "Of course."

The day dragged by. With no input from my friends, I felt left out and alone. At last I was able to resurrect myself from the quicksand and looked at the wall clock—ten minutes to quitting time.

Since our boss, Molly Rasmussen, was out of the office, she wouldn't be aware of me slipping out a few minutes early. I was eager to talk face-to-face with my cohorts to decide where we were in the data collection process.

* * *

On the way home, I called Dennis and invited him to join us and to ask our FBI liaison to be there as well. Dennis arrived and said Montgomery Williams begged off saying he was meeting with his superiors for a strategy planning meeting.

There was a crowd around the dinner table and lots of chatter. Sergeant York was having trouble keeping track of everyone. She figured it was her job to be certain everyone was identified and in their proper place. How she made such a determination was beyond me, but after three full circles of the table, she curled up on the doggie pad in the corner.

Aaron and Effie put out cold cuts and left-over's, and set it up as a buffet. Everyone filled a plate and returned to the dinner table. Dennis took the lead and relayed a message from the FBI. They were satisfied with all the evidence we had gathered, but there were still links missing. Alex found the deposit slip to the bank account they used and could testify about the link to Chet Peterson. The FBI would like us to link that bank account to others in the group. "Any ideas of how we tie others to that particular account?"

I felt like there was a light bulb over my head as the idea presented itself to me. "Assuming all the top players have access to the account, we may be able to draw them out," I said. "Wow, that got everyone's attention."

Everybody at the table stopped eating and looked at me. They were waiting for more.

"We know they will be operating under assumed names when they wrap this caper up. What if we can smoke them out using emails?" I noticed several at the table were giving me a "tell us more" look. "I sure don't know how to do it, but I bet CrackerJack would. If he can trace their normal email accounts and link them to another email name and account, we might solve two of the problems we have left."

Dennis stood and I thought he was coming around the table to me. Mistake. He headed to the kitchen and returned with a reloaded plate.

So much for being the center of attention.

"How would that solve two problems, and what are they?" Aaron said.

"We need their alias names. The link of two accounts would solve that mystery." I took a sip of wine and looked around the table before I continued. "If we, that's a royal 'we' because we need CrackerJack to carry out the details. If we can get an email to the main players telling them they will need to be able to identify themselves to get money out of their covert bank account. The email would ask them to come up with a five-digit code, like a PIN number, as an identifier. When they respond, we will have their names, aliases and a link to the account."

Effie jumped up. "Casey, I think that's a brilliant plan."

"I'll get in touch with CrackerJack today," I said. "If he's not too busy, we may have something by tonight."

52

I CONTACTED CRACKERJACK AND HE SAID HE COULD get the job done today. He promised to call me this evening at home.

The usual boring routine filled most of the day. I did manage to be productive for a portion of my time at work. That upset me, because I prefer to give more than a fifty-percent effort.

At five forty-five, I began to gather my belongings when Janet raced back into the office.

"I think I have a lead," she said.

I don't need this now. Not when I only want to get out of here. "What sort of lead?"

I turned to retrieve my purse, and when I looked for Janet she was gone. I hurried out the door to our office, but Janet was not to be seen in the hallway either. *So much for a hot lead.*

Nearing the exit to the hospital, I heard my name whispered. I was having a problem deciding what direction the sound came from. At last I saw a door that was ajar and I moved toward it.

"Casey, it's me Janet. In here." The door opened a bit more.

I poked my head into the opening and said, "So what's the big deal? Why all the cloak-and-dagger measures?"

"I didn't want any of the staff to see us prowling around the hospital after hours."

"Okay," I said. "What's the big deal you found?"

Janet shuffled her feet and looked down. "I think I've found out how those two women and the guy were killed."

"Great, let's get to it." I was mulling over her comment: two women and one man…Sam, died recently and he wasn't on our radar much before that. *How the hell does Janet know about him this quickly?*

"I got a couple of colas, want one?" Janet said.

"Yeah. Where are we headed?" I couldn't figure out if she was stalling or just nervous.

She handed me a can of pop. "Thanks for opening that pull tab; I almost always break a nail getting those dumb cans open."

Janet turned and started down the hall. "C'mon, we need to get up to the roof."

We moved toward the elevators that would take us to the top floor. From there we would need to climb only one flight of stairs. "How do we get through the door to the roof? I think they're locked," I said.

"No need to worry. My two WitSec guys will help us."

I nodded and lifted the cola can toward my mouth. *Beware of Greeks bearing gifts*—Alex's warning played in my head. With the can pressed to my lips, I tilted it up without allowing any of the liquid to enter my mouth. When I lowered, the can, I wiped my mouth with the back of my hand. Janet turned a corner, and before she was again in sight, I held the can so half of it spilled onto the tile floor.

In the elevator, I repeated my "drinking" sequence. Janet exited first and I dumped another healthy glug of the soda in the elevator. Her confederates were waiting when we reached the stairs to the roof.

The four of us trooped up the stairway, and one of the dudes unlocked the door to the roof. We stepped through and our shoes crunched on the gravel covered asphalt.

Ape Number One said, "Let me have that can."

I started my drinking routine again. Before the container reached my face, he snatched the can from my hand and handed it to Ape Number Two. Number Two hefted the can, gauging the weight. "She drank at least half…that ought to be plenty." Number One stepped behind me and put his paws on my shoulders. He turned toward the edge of the roof which was about thirty yards away.

Janet moved close to me and whispered in my ear. "Casey, we have a job to do. We need to get down to the parking lot. All you have to do is walk straight ahead. At the edge of the roof, just keep walking. It'll be okay, you can fly. Fly on down. I'll meet you down there."

Number One gave me a gentle shove, and I began walking. I took a few halting steps and heard the roof door slam shut. I walked a dozen more steps before I glanced over my shoulder to be sure Janet and the Apes were no longer on the roof.

I used my cell phone and dialed Falcon. I gave him an abbreviated version of these latest events. The crunching of my footsteps seemed so loud I was sure people at ground level could hear me coming. I sidled down the stairway, deciding to avoid the elevators. At the next floor landing, I saw my soda can. Seemed like the goon dropped it rather than dispose of it. "Littering will get you in trouble, my friend." I pulled a left-over Ziploc bag from lunch—good thing I'm cheap—to protect the can. *Now we would be able to test the can for fingerprints and toxins.*

I stayed in the shadows of a portico waiting. When I saw Falcon's car ease to the curb, I walked to the car as fast as I could without running. I made it to Falcon's car without being spotted by anyone—as best as I could tell.

"What the blue blazes have you been up to?" Falcon said.

I described the events in detail, Janet's instructions to me and the soda can. I thought of your comment concerning Greeks when Janet handed me the opened can and I took precautions."

"You didn't drink it, did you?"

"When I put it to my lips, I kept my mouth shut as tight as I could. I wiped my lips with my hand to reduce any residue of the cola. I don't think I ingested any of it. After each so-called *drink*, I dumped a slug of it out on the floor. Must have worked because one of the guys with Janet thought I drank at least half." I held up the plastic bag so Falcon could see the empty can.

"Good job, Casey. We'll test it for scopolamine. So, Janet told you that you could fly, did she?"

"Yeah. I guess that idea on top of the drug got three people to do a swan dive off the roof."

Falcon drove to the parking lot following my instructions. We pulled up in front of the Mustang. I reached for the door handle and paused.

"You do want to get your car, don't you?"

"No. I have an idea that may put the fear of God into Janet and her punks. Leave the car here and take me home."

We covered the ride to my place in silence.

* * *

Back at my condo, I revisited the entire story for Aaron and Effie. As I finished, Effie said, "What are you going to do tomorrow?"

"Funny you should ask. I'm going to go to the hospital early and be sitting at my desk when Janet walks in."

"Love your sense of the macabre," Falcon said.

Aaron was smiling and looking at the ceiling as if imagining the reaction, I would get from Janet.

* * *

We settled in to watch the late news when the phone rang. "Sure hope it's CrackerJack," I said. "He promised to have some news for me tonight."

CrackerJack apologized for the late call, but what he told me was reason enough to excuse his tardiness. He explained the details of his activities for the day, and we signed off.

"Come on, give," Aaron said.

"This will blow your hats off," I said. "First of all, CrackerJack pinned down the regular email accounts for all the players. If we want to, we could hack into any or all of them. That's big enough, but here's the topper. They all have access to a secret email account that doesn't leave a trail of emails in their wake."

"How can you avoid a trail of emails?" Effie said.

"Because the emails are never sent. All you need is an account at one of the big servers like Hotmail, Yahoo! or Gmail or the like. Everyone has the email account name and password. When you log on, you create the message and save it to the Draft folder. After a message has been read by everybody, the one in the Draft folder is deleted. No email is ever sent."

We decided this news called for a glass of wine.

Aaron rose and said, "I'll get a bottle from the fridge and glasses. Say, did you ever notice that nearly everything around here calls for a glass of wine?"

Knowing head nods and smiles all around.

Back at the dining room table, Effie said, "Are you going to send that email to everyone like you said?"

"It's already in the works." I said. "When I was on the phone with CrackerJack he asked me if I wanted to go ahead with the idea. I told him to go for it, so I imagine the bad guy grapevine is humming."

The three of us raced to the computer. I couldn't resist taking a look at the account. I logged in using the information CrackerJack gave me earlier. There it was, the Draft folder. I clicked on its icon and saw a short list of messages. After we read the notes inside, we were disappointed. Not much to hang on the lot of them, but enough to tie several names to the plots we were investigating.

With all the information CrackerJack accumulated and the evidence our group put together, I thought it was time to begin to roll up bad guys. Even though it was late, I put a call into Dennis.

He sounded a bit groggy when he answered. "Hi," I said. "I think it's time for some arrests."

"What do you mean, Casey?" he said.

I gave him the short version of where we were and asked him to record the rest of our conversation.

"Why do I need to do that?"

"Because I'm going to be talking fast and I don't want to repeat myself. Do you agree it's time to start making arrests?"

"Yeah, I suppose so. It may be tough to get warrants this time of night, but between me and the FBI, we should be able to pull it off. When we finish, I'll get on the horn and bring Montgomery up to speed. The Feds should be able to cut through some of the red tape and help with the warrants."

"Is the tape recorder running?" Dennis said it was and I began the litany of information, names, emails addresses, account numbers as well as dates that would substantiate many of the transactions. I told Dennis about my meeting with Janet I was planning and suggested we begin the arrests with her.

"Casey, I'm not sure that's a wise course. But if you're adamant, let's set nine a.m. as a time."

I wasn't sure I could wait that long, but I told Dennis it was okay. "Do you have an address for the two Marshalls?"

"I think Janet will roll on them and provide us with that information. Besides, we're not sure they are actually involved," Dennis said.

After my call to Dennis, I contacted the rest of our group to give them a heads-up. No one would have an active role, but I didn't want anyone blundering into an ongoing tactical situation. No use inviting trouble; the arresting officers would have enough on their minds without civilians in the way.

Becca was the most put out. "Dang. I was hoping you'd need my high-speed driving skills."

Alex and Falcon volunteered to be available. I thanked each of them, but said I doubted there would be any need since the cops and the Feds would be making the arrests. I neglected to tell them about the meeting I planned for Janet in the morning. What could go wrong with that?

53

THE NEXT MORNING, I WAS THINKING ABOUT meeting Janet at work. The exhilaration of confronting her pumped me up. And at the same time I wondered if something could go wrong. *What could possibly go wrong?*

A glance at the clock told me I had over an hour before the alarm would sound. Get up or pull the covers over my head and go for a few last minutes of sleep. I opted for the extra sleep, but it was a waste of time. My mind kept replaying the upcoming morning's challenge. I was confident the outcome would be positive and at the same time I had a sense of foreboding.

My mind raced until I thought I might need an aspirin. I squinted hard and pulled myself upright in bed. that the movement was enough to insure Sergeant York took my actions as an invitation. She was on me like a flash.

I flipped the comforter over her and we faux wrestled for a couple of minutes. She freed herself and looking satisfied, tipped her head and gave a short bark. "Okay," I said, "I'm up. Let's brush our teeth."

After breakfast, I started for the front door when I heard Sergeant York's nails clicking on the floor. I looked around in time to see her slide to a stop near my right leg. She took the hem of my pant leg in her mouth and tugged. I scolded her in my most indignant voice. Didn't work. Sergeant York pulled hard enough I figured if I didn't relent, I could expect the sound of ripping fabric.

I turned and stepped back toward my room. Sergeant York relaxed her grip and followed me into my bedroom. I stood still trying to figure out what my dog wanted me to do. My eyes fell on the shelf where I keep my purses. *It's legal to carry. This might be a good day to take the Glock along.*

I grabbed my purse with the built-in holster and tossed it on the bed. Sitting on the comforter, I loaded everything from the purse I picked out first into this one. I moved to my dresser and retrieved my Glock. I got two magazines from the drawer below. One mag went into the butt of the automatic. I racked the slide to put a round into the chamber. I slid the gun and the extra magazine in the "holster" section of the purse.

Walking back to the front door, Sergeant York jogged along beside me like I had issued a "heel" command. I did my best to understand what just happened. The only difference between a dog tugging on my pants and walking beside me is a different purse with my Glock inside. Could that be it?

I shook my head. "No way. Sergeant York, you can't be that smart…can you?"

She gave me a sharp bark, turned around and trotted back into the living room leaving me alone with my hand on the front doorknob.

* * *

The office was dark when I arrived. I decided to leave the lights off, and made my way to my desk. I draped my coat over the back of the chair and let my eyes adjust to a lack of light. I looked at Mickey Mouse on my wrist and he said I had twenty-five minutes before I could expect to see my co-workers show up.

I passed the time going over my stint here at the hospital, from the day I walked in and met what we believe to be the head of the fraud, Harriet Manfriedy, to CrackerJack's latest discovery about the email system they were using. I imagined Janet's recoil at seeing me here in the office; she would be expecting news of another person's demise. That should put her off guard. I ticked over a couple more facts that would help me keep her off guard in the hope she would fall apart and confess. I figured a confession would also finger the others in the plot.

Molly, my boss, came into the office and went to her desk. Rather than turning on the overhead lights, she flicked the switch on her desk lamp. Molly gave no indication she saw me sitting at my desk in the shadows.

My mind wandered and my lack of sleep caused me to doze while sitting there. A noise stirred my reverie and I jerked awake. Someone was in the office and I was afraid I was losing my advantage of surprise. My cell phone vibrated in my pocket. The caller ID said Alex was calling me.

"Casey, are you alone?" His voice was breathless.

"I'm in my office and the boss just came in. Why?"

"Casey, you need to get out of there. Now!" There was an insistence in his voice.

54

I FROWNED AS I LISTENED TO ALEX'S WORDS. "WHAT'S the matter?" I said into the phone.

"I just learned that those two goons who dog Janet aren't, I repeat, are *not* U.S. Marshalls. They have nothing to do with the WitSec program. I think that makes them even more dangerous than I thought before. Get out of there!"

Noises at the front of the office caught my attention. "Too late," I said. "I'll contact you later."

I slung my purse over my shoulder and stood. I eased my way toward the door of our office, doing my best to stay in the shadows. Janet came through the doorway. My appearance did have the affect I was hoping for. She recoiled with her eyes wide.

She recovered and said, "Well, Casey, what are you doing here? I expected to be reading your obituary this morning."

Even though she seemed composed, I figured her confusion still gave me an edge. I put a hand on her chest and pushed her to the side, expecting I could force my way past her. That was more than I could hope for. She did a sidestep, and the Ape Twins popped up just behind her. They pinned my arms to my sides and hustled me forward out of the office. I hoped our boss, Molly Rasmussen, would notice the activity and raise the alarm.

For the moment, I forgot Molly was part of the whole mess. If she noticed, she did not appear to be aware of our scuffle. The weight of my purse pulled down on the shoulder strap. I thought of the contents and tried to remember. *Did I ever mention my gun to Janet?* I didn't think so; I might still have an edge.

The three of them began to move me away from the pharmacy office. I wasn't sure where they would be taking me. Since it would be hard to force me to drink their special Kool-Aid, I ruled out the roof. Tossing a struggling body off a roof would leave marks they didn't want.

I recognized the hallway we were in. It led to the receiving dock and outside. Our gang was sure the bad guys had someone working here that was part of the fraud and scam. We were never able to pinpoint the person. Maybe this kidnapping attempt would help identify the missing conspirator. *Casey, you'd best pay attention to getting away from these yahoos instead of concentrating on that puzzle.*

"Where we going to take her?" one of the Apes said.

Janet thought for a minute. "Back to my place, I suppose. You got any better ideas?"

The Twin Apes shook their heads in unison. I wondered if their knuckles did touch the ground.

I took this second of distraction to break away. I ran to what seemed to be the office for the dock manager. Hunkering down behind the desk gave me a couple of minutes cover before my enemies could locate me.

When I entered the office on the receiving dock, I looked for anything that might be of help. On the desktop, I found a large rubber band. The cross section of the band was about a quarter of an inch across, and I remembered a game we used to play as kids. Stretch the band out, write letters on it and then release the tension. With the rubber band relaxed, the printing looked like several lines running close together. We would try to guess the message, then re-stretch the band to read the words. Using the rubber band and a ballpoint pen, I hurried to create my message and then slipped the band onto my wrist. I planned to wrap in around a lipstick as an anchor.

My message on this rubber band was: C H E Z J A N E T

From computer code writing habit I put the cross stroke on the "Z" so it wouldn't be confused with the number two. And *chez* is about the only word of French I remember from high school. It was the easiest and shortest reference to Janet's home I could think of. Help coming would depend on two things—first, my group would find the lipstick case with the rubber band wrapped around it and second…they would be able to decipher the message.

* * *

The first to arrive was a man named Matt. I congratulated myself on my deductive powers. Of course, the name tag sewn to his shirt which read MATT was a dead give-away.

One of the Apes was right behind Matt and said, "We'll take care of her."

"It'll be good riddance," Matt said.

Before they could drag me from the office, I saw the man's nameplate on his desk: Matthew Lewis. *Looks like we know the name of the guy down here who's in on the plot. Hope I get a chance to tell someone.*

Matt nodded and shoved me toward the Apes who hustled me down the steps from the dock to the parking level. Ape One said, "Which car should we take?"

"We'll take hers. That way it'll look like she left on her own. Where you parked, kiddo?"

At first, I resisted. After repeated threats, I gave them directions to my car, which is what I wanted. Weaving through the parking lot gave me the opportunity to fake several stumbles. My *ineptitude* allowed me to locate the lipstick in my purse, and I managed to wrap the large rubber band around the lipstick case several times so it wouldn't slip off. I kept the lipstick palmed in my hand.

Arriving at the Mustang, I did my best to shrug off Apes, and said, "I'll drive." I started to reach for my purse. "I've got my keys right here."

The Twins pulled the right door open, pushed the passenger seat back forward and forced me into the backseat. They were so forceful I banged a shin on the rocker panel. I moaned, reached for my leg and overplayed the scene. During my Act I, I was able to drop the lipstick and let it roll under the car.

One of the Apes shoved his way into the backseat with me while the other climbed behind the wheel. That left the "suicide" seat for Janet. The Ape behind the wheel said, "Gimme the keys," and reached over the seat back for my purse. I hung onto the strap in a feeble attempt to keep it from him. The force applied was more than needed and it almost jerked my arm out of its socket. Again, I overacted and moaned, holding my shoulder.

The man behind the wheel rummaged through the purse and came up with a set of keys. "You aren't much of a gentleman, asshole," I said to him. He slammed the purse back into the rear seat and I got another chance to act out. My words and the acting worked, no one seemed concerned that I was back in possession of my purse—and my gun.

I knew the general location of Janet's house from our previous snooping. Our direction of travel confirmed my thoughts. We were headed toward the northern edge of Little Rock just west of the area referred to as the Heights.

I twisted a bit in the seat so I could cast a furtive glance out the rear window. It took two attempts to gain my objective. As I turned the second time, the Ape in the backseat with me grabbed my arm. "What the hell you looking at?" He twisted me back straight in the seat and leaning forward, he said to the driver, "You got any suspicious cars behind us?"

Driver Ape said, "Nah. I been watching the rearview and ain't seen nothing."

Janet looked at the driver and then at us in the rear seat. "Calm down, guys. Casey, are you expecting someone to follow us?"

I kept my mouth shut. Since it would take a while for members of our group to pick up the scent, I wasn't expecting anyone soon. My purpose was to increase the jumpy feelings my captors had. I got the desired results; all three of them kept checking mirrors and the back window.

I gauged my chances of getting to my automatic in the near time. I ruled it out for the moment; too close quarters and not sure I could control the circumstances well enough. The most confusing and uncoordinated period might be as we exited the car at Janet's place.

For now…wait and see.

55

THE MUSTANG PULLED TO A STOP IN FRONT OF A two-story home which I figured must belong to Janet. I steeled myself as the passenger door opened and Janet reached for the seat back. My backseat companion squeezed his way out and turned to watch me exit. I struggled being as clumsy as I could. When I gained my feet outside the car, I judged the conditions.

The Ape and Janet were standing a few feet apart and the second Ape was still by the driver's door. *Now or never*…I lowered my head slightly and charged toward the space between the Ape and Janet.

For a moment, I thought was going to make it. Wrong! The guy slammed what must have been a fist into my back as I sprang between the two. I sprawled, face down, on the grassy area between the curb and the sidewalk. The two guys grabbed my arms and pulled me upright between them. I staggered along as Janet said, "I'd better get her car out of sight. Use this key to get in the house and give me the car keys."

They all did their jobs and I was soon inside the house. It was an older two-story in good condition. Inside, I did my best to make detailed observations about the place. Beautiful hardwood floors gleamed with wax, and rugs covered most of the bare floor. Dated wallpaper gave a hint to the home's age. On the way up the staircase I continued my stumble number and one of the goons grabbed the purse from my shoulder. At the top of the stairs, I saw a hallway and several doors. I assumed one of them was a bathroom and the others bedrooms.

I was pushed toward a door to my left that was opposite the stairway. As I passed, I noticed the door on the right was not as wide as the other doors—probably a closet. A large sliding bolt type lock had been added to the outside of the door to "my" room.

A hand on my back propelled me forward. Inside my prison, I heard the door slam behind me and the bolt slam home. I walked to the window and looked out. The lot sloped down toward the back and the drop from this window to the ground was closer to three stories than two. Bare walls with only one door besides the entry. It turned out to be a small clothes closet, which was bare…not even a coat hanger. The two small throw rugs had seen far better days and added to the *old* odor in the room. A ladder-back chair was the only furnishing in sight.

They had my purse and gun, leaving me with little to work with.

I sat on the lone chair and considered my present situation. The window was no doubt too far to the ground. Even if I landed well, the odds of spraining an ankle or worse yet, breaking something, were too much of a gamble. Nothing like escaping from this room only to be disabled on the ground below. I thought about the clue I left for those who might be coming after me.

I crossed the room and began a grid search to be sure I knew everything available to me—precious little. As I passed the small throw rug, I picked it up looking for something I could use— nothing. I finished my sweep of the room and returned to the straight back chair.

As I sat there, a plan began to form in my head. I would pull off a fake break out that would give me the opportunity to make a real escape. I considered the small closet in the room, but discarded the idea. That would be the first place anyone would look. The window I was facing jumped out at me as the perfect decoy.

I went over the details in my head at least five times. I wanted a mental diagram planted in my head so I could execute each step without thinking. Satisfied the plan could work, now I needed to stage the room and set the plan in motion.

* * *

I pressed an ear to the hallway door and the voices of all three coming from downstairs were loud enough to make out. Janet was issuing commands to both of her cohorts. The instructions directed one of the Apes to place a chair near the bottom of the stairs so the door to my room was visible.

From the sounds, I was convinced they would not do a physical check on me for some time. In an ideal situation, early morning, say around four to five, is the best time to catch people sleeping and off guard. I doubted I could wait until tomorrow morning.

I picked up the small rug and examined it again. Typical of this type of floor covering, the underside was a rubberized material to keep it from slipping on slick surfaces. I folded a corner three times to form a triangle with the rubberized side out. I forced the corner into the space between the bottom of the door and the floor so the rug would act as a door jam and keep it from opening. A stubborn door should give my kidnappers something to ponder and delay their entrance.

My captors left me with my personal belongings other than my purse. I checked my Mickey Mouse and it was half past ten. I decided to wait until quarter to twelve to make my move. I leaned back in the chair, got as comfortable as I could and waited.

I put my watch up to my ear to see if Mickey was still ticking. He was and I resigned myself to the wait. I slumped in the chair, closed my eyes and did my best to rest. After three minutes in the *rest* position, I was on my feet again. I paced the perimeter of the room to work off some of the excess energy.

Another glance at my watch said I there was another hour to wait. I resumed my pacing, all the while rehearsing the steps of my plan. I rechecked the window to be certain I could open it, easing it up a half inch and closing it again. My eyes searched the sill, side frames, and the bottom half of the double hung window. No nails in sight that could prevent me from opening it all the way.

I stood next to the hinge side of the door to this room and checked angles of view for the lebendy-seventh time. I swung my arm, simulating the view someone standing by the window would have of the door to the closet. Nothing changed since the last time I went through the drill.

I managed to spend an inordinate amount of time this latest chore. Inordinate, maybe, however it used up a bunch of my *wait* time. At twenty-three minutes before midnight, I decided it was time to put my plan in motion.

"Damn." The expletive leapt from my mouth. *How the hell could I have missed the most important part of the plan?*

56

THERE I WAS, ALL DRESSED UP AND NO PLACE TO GO. In all my planning, I neglected the most important step—the initial one. How am I going to get my captors to initiate a search for me? I can't shout, *hey, guys, come look for me!* I needed an action which would get their attention without giving away the fact I wanted them to come looking.

I sat in the chair searching my mind for a way to attract my captors. My eyes were heavy and I weighed the value of a nap. I was close to convincing myself a short nap was in order. I let my eyelids close.

The scuffling at the door wasn't loud, but loud enough to rouse me.

"I've got some lunch for you." It was Janet's voice and I could hear her fumbling with the doorknob.

I think she's forgotten the slide bolt I saw as they ushered me in here. The bolt was up toward the top of the door. I couldn't wait. I shot out of the chair being careful not to make noises that would give me away. For my plan to work, I needed them to think I escaped the room.

As I moved to the window, I checked to be sure the small rug was still jammed under the door to the room—it was. I slid the lower half of the window up as far as it would go, turned and hurried back to the wall next to the entryway to the room. Janet was still struggling with the bolt. I pressed my back to the wall and edged as close to the hinge jamb as possible.

I got ready for the door to swing open. Janet slammed the exterior bolt to the open position making a good bit of noise.

I could tell she now had her hand on the doorknob. She eased the door open about three inches and then gave it a shove. The folded rug did its job and slowed her progress. I let her struggle for a moment and then kicked the rug loose. The door slammed open and I caught the handle to keep it from rebounding. It was hiding me in the V space formed by the wall and the open door.

Standing in my place of concealment, I could not see the window or the closet door. I hoped the opposite view was as limited as mine.

"I think she jumped out the window," Janet said in a voice loud enough to attract the two guys who were apparently still on the lower floor.

The sound of the feet pounding up the stairs grabbed my attention. The two Apes made straight for the window.

One of the Apes roared a couple of expletives.

"That's a long damn way down," said the second Ape. "How'd she survive the leap without breaking something?"

I continued holding the door tight against me and doing my best to control my breathing.

"Aw, hell. She didn't jump," Ape One said. "She's in that damn closet."

I heard hinges squeak and then the closet door smashed into the wall. "She ain't in here…it's empty," said Ape Two.

"For crap's sake, Janet. Put the damn tray down." He was grumbling the words and I couldn't tell who said it. He continued, "Let's get round to the backyard and see if we can pick up her trail."

Music to my ears. Their actions were following my plan script so far. As soon as I heard them on the stairs, I eased from behind the door—room empty…upper hall empty. I eased out of my room and saw the three exiting the front door. I waited what I estimated to be half a minute and then moved, being as quiet as I could be while I eased down the staircase.

I reached the bottom and discovered another plan-point I missed. The front door was set with a heavy deadbolt lock—the type that needed a key on the inside as well as outside. Logic told me a key for the lock would be nearby—after all, who wants to be trapped during an emergency and no way to open the front door from the inside? Probably correct, but useless. I knew I didn't have time to locate the hidey-hole where the key resided.

At this point, my only saving grace was the closet by the front door. I heard heavy footsteps on the front porch.

Combining caution and speed I hoped this door wasn't a *squeaker*. My luck held; I was in the closet without making noise before the front door was shoved open. There wasn't the sound of anyone fumbling with keys in the lock and I was left with a disappointing proposition. Since they were in a hurry on the way out, they didn't bother locking that dead bolt. I gave myself a virtual forehead smack...if I'd tried the door, it would have opened.

Too late, because now there was the sound of a deadbolt being locked. One more stumbling block. I edged back into a corner of the closet and my foot bumped something on the floor. Most doors let in light, but this one was light tight. Curses on the builder. I did my best to figure the object out, but my foot wasn't sensitive enough. I bent and tentatively extended my hand.

The first object my fingers located was a strap. It felt familiar. Further examination confirmed my initial impression. I stumbled on my missing purse. My spirits soared for the first time since I put my plan into motion. I picked it up and examined the contents—special compartment first. I was giddy. My Glock still snuggled in its holster. I felt ten feet tall.

I could hear the three of them talking in the living room. The discussion—more of an argument—centered on me and how I could have eluded them. I could almost see them pointing fingers at one another. They found no footprints on the ground beneath the window.

"Yeah, but the ground's kind of hard. Maybe she lit and rolled," said one of the men.

Janet spoke next. "Nothing looked disturbed. I think she's still in the house."

"How the hell did she get out of the room without us seeing her?" the second man said.

The conversation subsided and I wondered if they were gone. No sound of them on the stairs, so I assumed they were still in the living room. Even though I now possessed my gun, the odds were still in their favor. Three to one and two of them armed. My best chance was escaping from the house.

The deadbolt posed a major obstacle. I tried to picture the area near the front door and a handy place to keep the key. There was a coat tree to the left of the door and a small occasional table to the right. *Was there a drawer in the table?* I couldn't remember one, but most tables do have a drawer.

When the three voices became faint, I was sure they were all on the second floor. I eased the closet door open and peeked out. I could see the stairs, and there was no sign of them. I took three quick steps to the table being careful not to make any noise. I only needed to open the drawer a few inches before I could see the key. It was on a short chain with an automotive fob. I pocketed the *treasure*, closed the drawer and slipped back into the closet. Now I felt in control of my future.

Casey, you're standing in a dark closet with three adversaries still milling around—two of them armed—isn't that feeling a bit optimistic?

I listened and could hear no sounds from upstairs. This might be my best shot at getting through the front door. I eased the closet door open an inch at a time, using each increment to search as much of the room and the stairs as I could. When the opening was wide enough for me to slip through, I moved into the room far enough to have a view of the full living room. To my surprise, Janet was sitting on a sofa about fifteen feet from me.

I leveled my Glock at her and put an index finger up to my lips. Instead of remaining quiet, she shouted, "HELP, HELP! She's down here in the living room." I heard footsteps thundering on the floor upstairs.

57

THE FIRST GUY APPEARED AT THE TOP OF THE STAIRS with a gun in his hand. I put a round into the wall just in front of him. I wasn't aiming at the wall, but that was the best I could do with a hurried shot. He ducked back and his arm swiveled toward me. I didn't have much cover from my position. The corner of the wall forming the foyer was not much cover; I couldn't maneuver to aim my fire.

He let loose with two quick shots and plaster flew from the wall near my head. A spray of white dust got in my eyes and gave me a coughing fit. So much for this plan. I began calculating the chances of getting to the door, using the deadbolt key, and exiting the house with all my parts intact. The figure I came up with was not encouraging, so I cast my mind to other possibilities. My mind was a blank.

I resorted to peeking around the corner to view the stairway, in time to see the second man dash further down the upstairs hall. He was too fast for me to take a shot at him. He now occupied another position with cover and a new angle of fire at me. It wasn't enough to see me when I was back from the corner of the foyer wall, however they were now in a position to keep me so busy I might not be able to continue firing at them. They could alternate taking potshots at me.

I tested my hypothesis and poked my head out far enough to take fire. Another spray of dust. By now, there must enough white dust on me I may well look like Grandma Moses. Before I could contemplate the extent of how bad off I was, there was a crash of glass from the window beside the front door, followed by a chair I remembered seeing on the porch when we arrived.

The chair was followed by an object I didn't recognize. It bounced once, twice and began its life's work. After the blinding light, an explosion followed and was so loud it set my head spinning and my ears ringing. *Flash—Bang* were the words my mind formed.

Looking back toward the now-shattered window remnants, a figure dove through the opening into the foyer area. The man rolled and came up to a shooting crouch—fired his weapon three times—then dove and rolled toward what little cover was available. The end of a sofa was little protection from the fusillade unleashed from the top of the stairs. It must have been enough to stop any bullets that were on target, because the figure rose and loosed a volley of three shots. This time I recognized the person as Falcon.

I edged from behind my cover with my weapon aimed at the top of the stairs. I was right; both men upstairs were visible and concentrating on Falcon. I fired two quick shots at each which diverted attention back to me. Again, both men exposed themselves and fired in my direction. I was already back behind my cover as the white dust drifted around me again. I heard two quick shots. I figured the last rounds fired were from Falcon, and my suspicions were confirmed when I saw him rise to a near standing position and move toward the stairs.

"I think I got both of them," Falcon said.

I stepped out into the living room and leveled my Glock at Janet who was in a new location, out of the field of fire, where she apparently moved during the gunfight. The overstuffed chair allowed enough room for her to cower in a near fetal position. "Just stay where you are, Janet," I said.

I moved to a position behind and to the right of Falcon to cover him as he climbed the stairs. I was halfway up when he reached the top. I watched him approach each of the perps, kick their guns aside, and check each for a pulse. "Easy, Casey," he said. "They're both down for the count."

I was still having trouble with my hearing, but I understood what he said. In the background, I heard another voice, shouting. "Falcon, get your ass back outside." It was Dennis.

I turned and shouted toward the front door. "Dennis, all clear! Two perps down and one in custody."

The next sound was of a heavy object smashing the front door open. I moved aside because I was in fear of the stampeding herd of officers flowing through the front door. I saw jackets and vests with, FBI, SWAT, POLICE, HRT and one more I wasn't able to read.

At Dennis' direction, a police officer escorted Falcon and me outside toward the front yard. We found Alex, Effie and Aaron milling in the street. We exchanged hugs along with congratulatory high-fives. "How did you find us?" I said to the group.

Aaron rushed into the gap. "Well, Falcon remembered where your car was parked…Effie spotted the lipstick case you dropped—"

Effie put an elbow to Aaron's chest, pushed him back and continued. "At first we didn't know why you put the rubber band around it. Then I remembered the game we played as kids—leaving notes on a stretched-out rubber band."

"We didn't get the message at first," Alex said. "We read it as CHE 2, and no one could make any sense out of it. Effie came to the rescue when she remembered seeing you write your Z's with the slash mark. That's when we thought of the little French we knew and headed for Janet's house."

"Let's get home," I said. "I owe Sergeant York a pile of treats."

We split into groups for the ride back. Aaron and Effie rode with me and Alex climbed in with Falcon.

* * *

We were congregating in the dining room and busy uncorking wine bottles. Sergeant York was clearly awed by the activity because she was nowhere in sight. Wine poured, we were sipping away when Falcon arrived.

"Where's Alex?" I said.

Falcon hefted a couple of packages wrapped in brown paper and tied with heavy twine. "He said you would know what these are, and he asked me to drop him at the airport."

I took the parcels and placed them on the table. "Yeah, I know. He said he wrote about a couple of adventures in his life." I took the note tucked under the cord on one of the packages and read it to the group. "Casey, you asked about my previous escapades, and these two 'books' will give you a good idea. Do with them what you may. I would be proud if you could get them published, but I fear they will need an atrocious amount of editing. Felicitations to your group and love to you. Alex."

I was flabbergasted to find Alex had already written two books. We unwrapped the parcels and discussed the possibility of going into the publishing business.

Sergeant York came tearing into the room and I stood up. I held out my arms, and she made a wild leap and landed in my arms. "Little girl," I said to her. "I owe you a bunch for dragging me around this morning until I loaded my gun into the purse."

I put her down, gave her the treats I promised earlier and watched her gobble them down. I looked up and silently thanked her again. "Come here, you scamp." I said.

Sergeant York ambled toward me and an image formed in my mind. I loved this little replacement for PK, but I still missed my Psycho Kitty. Then I had an image of PK sitting by The Rainbow Bridge waiting for me. That took the pain away…well, most of the pain.

THE END

READER REVIEWS ABOUT THE PREVIOUS CASEY FREMONT MYSTERIES:

One, Two – Kill a Few

My three girls gave me a Kindle a few days before I got your email. Your book was my first purchase. One, Two - Kill a Few is great! I mean it!! It is an attention grabbing, don't want to put it down kind of book.

GLYNDA B.

John Achor draws the audience into the mystery immediately with "raining bodies." The reader's curiosity is hooked as the story progresses with the addition of friends to help solve the mystery. A growing romance with the police detective holds the reader's attention as the killers are tracked through the evolving story. I enjoyed every page and would recommend it to all who read mysteries. I'm looking forward to more Casey Fremont books. Thank you, Mr. Achor.

RITA D.

and *Three, Four – Kill Some More*

As with his first novel, John's second effort makes a great read. It is fast paced, with interesting twists & turns in the plot. I look forward to John's third novel (which I understand he is hard at work writing.)

BOB M.

My new friend, Casey, is in more trouble. Big trouble. Luckily she has a good posse to help her out. I was hoping she'd survive again so someday I can read *Five, Six – Deadly Mix*. Once again, couldn't put the book down til I finished it.

CARLENE W.

APPENDIX

HERE ARE THE THREE PIECES OF PAPER DR. JAY GAVE TO CASEY.

THE RAINBOW BRIDGE

Just this side of heaven is a place called The Rainbow Bridge.

When an animal dies that has been especially close to someone here, that pet goes to The Rainbow Bridge.

There are meadows and hills for all of our special friends so they can run and play together.

There is plenty of food, water and sunshine, and our friends are warm and comfortable.

All the animals who had been ill and old are restored to health and vigor; those who were hurt or maimed are made whole and strong again, just as we remember them in our dreams of days and times gone by.

The animals are happy and content, except for one small thing; they each miss someone very special to them, who had to be left behind.

They all run and play together, but the day comes when one suddenly stops and looks into the distance. His bright eyes are intent; His eager body quivers. Suddenly he begins to run from the group, flying over the green grass, his legs carrying him faster and faster.

You have been spotted, and when you and your special friend finally meet, you cling together in joyous reunion, never to be parted again. The happy kisses rain upon your face; your hands again caress the beloved head, and you look once more into the trusting eyes of your pet, so long gone from your life but never absent from your heart.

Then you cross Rainbow Bridge together…

—Author unknown…

LAST NIGHT

I stood by your bed last night; I came to have a peep.
I could see that you were crying you found it hard to sleep.
I whined to you softly as you brushed away a tear,
"It's me, I haven't left you, I'm well, I'm fine, I'm here."
I was close to you at breakfast, I watched you pour the tea,
You were thinking of the many times, your hands reached
down to me.
I was with you at the shops today; your arms were getting sore.
I longed to take your parcels; I wish I could do more.
I was with you at my grave today; you tend it with such care.
I want to reassure you, that I'm not lying there.
I walked with you toward the house, as you fumbled for
your key.
I gently put my paw on you; I smiled and said, "it's me."
You looked so very, tired and sank into a chair.
I tried so hard to let you know, that I was standing there.
It's possible for me, to be so near you every day.
To say to you with certainty, "I never went away."
You sat there very quietly, then smiled, I think you knew…
in the stillness of that evening, I was very close to you.
The day is over…I smile and watch you yawning
and say "goodnight, God bless, I'll see you in the morning."
And when the time is right for you to cross the brief divide,
I'll rush across to greet you and we'll stand, side by side.
I have so many things to show you, there is so much for you
to see.
Be patient, live your journey out…then come home to be
with me.
　　—Author unknown…

THE CAT 10 COMMANDMENTS

Submitted by the Fitzsimmons Army Medical Center— Published by the SPCA of Pinellas County. FL. From Cornell University Cat Watch Newsletter.

1. My life is likely to last 10 to 15 years, any separation from you will be painful for me. Remember that before you get me.

2. Give me time to understand what you want from me.

3. Place your trust in me. It is crucial to my well-being.

4. Don't be angry with me for long, and don't lock me up as punishment. You have your work, entertainment and friends. I only have you.

5. Talk to me sometimes. Even if I don't understand your words, I understand your voice.

6. Be aware that however you treat me, I'll never forget.

7. Please don't hit me. I can't hit back, but I can bite and scratch and I really don't want to do that.

8. Before you scold me for being uncooperative obstinate, or lazy ask yourself if something might be bothering me. Perhaps I'm not getting the right foods or I've been in the sun too long or my heart is getting old and weak.

9. Take care of me when I grow old. You too will grow old.

10. Go with me on difficult journeys. Never say, "I can't bear to watch or let it happen in my absence." Everything is easier for me if you are there.

Remember, I LOVE you too.

ABOUT THE AUTHOR

John Achor's writing assignments have appeared in various local, national and international publications such as *Good Old Days, Computer Pilot, The Storyteller* and *Writers' Journal.* He enjoys writing about, "The subjects I know best: the military, flying and people I've known." After that, John says he lets a vivid imagination take over.

The first of his three careers spanned twenty years as a U.S. Air Force pilot. He accumulated over 4,000 hours flying planes from Piper Cubs to the military equivalent of the Boeing 707.

After the military, he entered the real estate industry. He joined a national real estate franchise as a management consultant working at the regional and national levels. Those positions led him to Phoenix, Arizona, and an affiliation with a major Savings & Loan institution.

In John's words, "When the Savings and Loan industry melted away like a lump of sugar in hot coffee, I knew it was time to develop a third career." He became a freelance computer instructor, user-developer, consultant, writer and Community College instructor.

In the 1990s, John began developing characters to fill ideas he had in mind for thrillers and mystery novels. The thriller series features Alex Hilliard, an Air Force pilot, and a thirty-something lady is the leading light in the Casey Fremont mystery series.

By the 2000s, he put five novels featuring Casey Fremont and Alex Hilliard in the can and launched his writing career. He and his wife left Arizona for Arkansas and later relocated to Nebraska. From there, John continues writing and has ideas in mind for a third thriller and has completed the first chapters of the fourth mystery novel.

ASSAULT ON THE PRESIDENCY

PREVIEW

From Casey's latest adventure, you learned about her uncle, Alex Hilliard. Alex left a pair of manuscripts with Casey, and after reading them she decided to publish them as a tribute to her Uncle Alex.

Here, I've included the Prologue from the first of those novels *Assault on the Presidency*.

AN ALEX HILLIARD THRILLER

BY JOHN ACHOR

PROLOGUE

NOVEMBER 11TH, THE PENTAGON

Only minutes ago, Lieutenant Colonel Alex Hilliard had folded his lanky frame into his Mustang. Now he eased his car to a stop before he departed the North parking lot. As he checked for traffic, he could see the building over his shoulder. The massive, gray outline of the Pentagon loomed behind him. An icy, prickly sensation crawled up his spine.

He realized that this would, in all likelihood, be the most important briefing he would ever give. *It's going to be a damn long night and day…twenty-four hours…drive two hundred and fifty miles one way; tell The Man a story that even I had trouble believing. The drive will be the easiest part. Telling him won't be that hard. Convincing him…that may take more time than I have. After that, all I have to do is retrace my steps and be back to work!*

* * *

Even studying for his doctoral dissertation, Alex found there was ample time for boredom in his job. He had managed to complete a Masters Degree during his previous assignment. He was fortunate that there had been an excellent program at the university located just eight miles from his base. Now it was time to push his education further. He enjoyed the challenge of learning and something in the back of his mind was telling him to go for it. It could be another punch on his ticket to future promotions. Alex was beginning to suspect that he had a sponsor who had helped him attain his current rank. There was havoc in the promotion process. Making lieutenant colonel usually wasn't the world's toughest feat, but reduced threats abroad and the resulting military drawdowns made it difficult. The year Alex was eligible for lieutenant colonel, there had been a half-dozen people qualified for every open slot on the promotion list. *If I do have a sponsor, I may as well give him more ammunition for the next go around*, Alex thought. So as soon as he settled into his Pentagon assignment, he looked for a good school where the Ph.D. program could fit his work schedule.

It was the boredom that paved the road to this evening; he wandered the halls and poked his nose into cubicles here and corners there. He looked, probed, and learned the myriad details that made the big building tick in the dark, quiet hours of the night.

* * *

It started innocently enough, just routine duties and looking for ways to pass the long hours on a dull shift. Alex's workspace was just off the National Military Command Center. The NMCC was on the second floor of the Pentagon, a structure that after more than four decades remained the world's largest office building. Just inside the River Entrance to the big building, teams assigned to the NMCC worked eight-hour shifts, rather than the twelve he worked. That upset Alex at first, but it did give him an overlap with them and he got to know more of the NMCC team members. The teams are comprised of representatives of all the services and the various civilian agencies that have an interest in intelligence gathering around the world.

The area where Alex worked was a good deal smaller and more cramped than the NMCC, but he did have the satisfaction of knowing that most of the folks next door weren't even allowed in these spaces. Part of his duties required him to deliver message traffic to the Cab in the NMCC. The Cab was the glass enclosure where the senior duty officer, a general or an admiral, sat with his aide. The Navy provided captains for the deputy position while the other services assigned colonels.

Alex also knew that when he delivered message traffic to the Cab there were only a handful of people over there who had the necessary clearances to read it.

Alex even felt a bit smug when he made these trips. He could move past dozens of people who outranked him and walk directly into the Cab. He would usually just gaze out over the panorama of the people staffing the duty desks, and the large screens representing the current situation throughout the world.

Occasionally someone he knew would catch his eye and their body language told him that they wanted to know what was up. Alex would shrug his shoulders as if to say, "Beats me" and turn back while the duty general finished reading the messages. The general would indicate whether he wanted a copy of the message for his "read-file" or whether he would simply enter the subject in his log. More times than not, they asked for a copy, so the daylight "wheels" could read it also.

* * *

There was something Alex couldn't put his finger on, but it continued to gnaw at him. Like waking in the morning and knowing that during the night you had dreamed. Try as you might, those snatches of the dream fighting their way to the conscious mind would drift away and leave that empty, frustrated feeling.

He felt the frustration. As if he knew something but didn't even know what it was that he knew. It wasn't there all the time, but occasionally Alex could feel it. It seemed so vague that he nearly dismissed it from his mind, but in the wee hours of a particularly dull work shift, it surged back into his mind. The feeling was akin to being caught in a wall of water rushing down a dry riverbed. It struck late one night. "There is something going on." Alex hadn't realized he verbalized his thoughts and the flood continued to fill his mind.

* * *

He drifted back over the years of flying. The times the bird didn't feel quite right; the strange noises an airplane can make, as if she's talking to you…telling you what is happening or about to happen. Telling you that it's time to pay attention or you'll be so far behind her mentally when the trouble starts, you'll never catch up.

It's seldom that one horrendous emergency gets you. It's not often a catastrophic failure occurs. More often, it's the cumulative effect of a dozen little kinks that you have ignored. In one blinding instant they all come together and if you haven't prepared yourself they will reach out, grab you by the throat, and choke the life out of you. The myriad details that happen, right or wrong; that put you and your airplane together at that particular instant in time, in that particular piece of the sky.

Sometimes it's the silence that sounds the warning. The humming and rumbling that should be there and isn't. Or the times when you think that your mind has wandered and that you haven't been scanning the gauges properly. They were all in-the-green and the subconscious recorded that fact, so why clutter the consciousness with such trivia.

Then there was the opposite reaction. Glance up to scan the dials and let just one of the needles, on all those gauges, point the wrong direction and a mental alarm bell sounds. The conscious mind is jerked to the reality of something out of place, and the adrenaline begins to pump.

* * *

Alex jerked himself back to the task at hand. *It's hard to believe that it's only been three weeks!* He wheeled his little coupe onto the freeway and headed south wondering what the next three weeks would bring.

END OF THE PROLOGUE

(Final edit may vary a bit from this excerpt. Stay tuned for the release of *Assault on the Presidency*, coming soon.)

BONUS MATERIAL ADDED
FOR THIS EDITION

Author's Note:
Second World printing rights. First World rights belong to the
Nebraska Writers Guild for publication of this short story in
their 2017 anthology *Voices from the Plains.*

THE OLD VICTORIAN
A TRILOGY

PART ONE: THE CLOSET

BILL PASSED THE DOOR AGAIN THINKING, ONE OF
these days. One of these days, I'll get the door to this closet
open. The object of his obsession was located in the hallway on
the second floor.

Bill and Sarah Ross moved into their home three weeks ago
after his company transferred him to this small town, Eureka
Springs, in northwest Arkansas. When they mentioned their turn-
of-the-century acquisition, they often found the term needed
refinement. "That's the turn of the 20th century, not 2001."

Sarah wanted the house, saying it was in the best school
district in the city. She said, "And this is the only house in the
neighborhood we can afford."

"Afford may not be the right term," Bill said. "We're going to have to stretch the budget to swing it."

The house needed a lot of work, but the electrical and heating-air conditioning systems were less than ten years old. An inspector assured them their one-hundred-year-plus Victorian home was sound and the foundation of the two-and-a-half story house was not likely to crumble or leak. Bill was dreading the day the exterior would need repainting. He couldn't imagine brandishing a paintbrush around all those knobs, newels and gee-gaws.

Being accustomed to wallboard construction, Bill found lath and plaster walls a major challenge. He did, after several aborted attempts, learn how to repair and patch his initial efforts at hanging pictures.

During the closing on the house, the real estate agent handed them a large iron ring with eleven keys attached. She pointed to the one marked FRONT, saying, "That opens the front door, but I'm afraid you'll have to experiment with the rest to find doors they match."

Another dang headache, Bill thought.

The couple discovered hideaways, and small rooms with sloped ceilings that matched the pitch of the roof, and more than ample closet space. Everywhere they turned they found niches, alcoves, recesses and cubbyholes where they could put their furniture as well as those seldom used objects. When they entered the small room with the creaky floor near their bedroom, Sarah said, "Wouldn't this make a cozy nursery? Whenever we get around to that."

Bill grinned.

There was no hurry to go into the frustrating closet, the one which defied entrance. But Bill tried every key on the iron ring given them—more than once—and not one would fit the lock. He knew it was more frustration than need driving him.

The idea came in a blinding flash like that lightbulb over the head of a cartoon character. Bill hurried to the kitchen pantry, a small room of its own, retrieved a hammer and screwdriver from his toolbox and hurried upstairs to The Closet. "Okay. Let's see how tough you are without hinges."

His plan was to knock out the hinge pins so he could pry the door away from the jam. Poised in front of the door, with tools at the ready, Bill's jaw went slack and his mouth fell open… there were no hinge pins visible. "I'll be…the door must open inward—in toward the closet. That's darn strange."

Bill started at the sound of Sarah's voice. "What are you mumbling about? What in the world are the tools for?"

He explained his idea and the dilemma facing him. "I may need to hire a carpenter to remove this door."

"We don't need the space, and…we certainly don't need the added expense right now. Forget about the door."

As usual, her logic was solid, but still…In the end he heeded her admonitions, but every time he passed his nemesis, a frown contorted his face and a muttered curse escaped his lips.

Late one night as he walked down the second-floor hallway, Bill thought he heard a noise emanating from the closet. Pressing an ear to the door, he closed his eyes to focus his hearing.

Nothing.

He stepped back and ran his eyes around the four edges of the door. He pressed his fingertips to the small crevices between door and jam. Too narrow for a grip. Bill straightened his body, looked around to be sure Sarah wasn't watching, reached out and knocked on the door—a light and timid tap and then he waited.

"It's about time. Come in."

Bill's eyes darted both directions looking for someone in the hall. No one…At last he said, "I can't. The door is locked."

A moment later he heard a lock click and saw the ornate doorknob turn. The door swung inward about twelve inches. The light from the hall did not penetrate the room beyond the portal.

"Come in," the voice said again.

"Can't you turn on a light first?" Bill said.

"No. Either come in or go away forever."

He pushed against the door, but it would not open any farther. Using all the courage he could summon, Bill made a half-turn and sidled partway through the narrow opening. Something gripped his arm and propelled him into the closet. The door closed with a quiet click.

He waited.

Silence.

He squinted, hoping his eyes would adjust to the blackness that shrouded him. Nothing.

Silence and an ebony blanket enveloped him. After an eternity, he said, "Okay. What now?"

Silence.

Bill felt behind him, located the doorknob. It would not turn.

His second attempt to communicate failed like the first. "I might as well see how big this closet is," he said hoping to draw out his host. He wondered if he was whistling past a graveyard.

Nothing.

He inched along keeping his back to the wall, tapping a foot to the side as he sidled along the wall. Don't want to fall through a hole in the floor, he thought. Moving in halting half steps, he counted each one figuring he could return to the door if he didn't find another way out…or his host.

Seventeen steps later, he encountered a wall running a different direction than the one behind his back. To his surprise, it was not a ninety-degree corner. Bill estimated the obtuse angle at one-hundred and twenty degrees, give or take. He reviewed the number of steps, the distance traveled, corner angle and did his best to estimate the size of the room. He remembered his geometry teacher berating the class for their feeble attempts to solve the problems. Wish I'd paid more attention in that class.

It struck him that any guess at the room size depended on there being some symmetry to this place. With all the weird stuff going on, I can't depend on that being true.

Bill decided to return to the closet door he entered and pound on it until Sarah heard him. She could call a carpenter, 9-1-1, or something to get him out of his self-induced predicament. His breath came in short gasps. Retracing his steps, he counted seventeen. Extending his arms both directions, he could feel no door. He backtracked a half-dozen paces—still no door. Bill moved forward the last six and six more steps feeling for the door all the way.

The oppressive silence and darkness chafed his nerves raw. He could feel walls closing in on him, sucking air from his lungs. Sliding to the floor, shivering, he wondered how to stave off claustrophobia. The blackness pressed against every cell of his body and his mind until he slipped into emptiness.

When consciousness returned, a pinprick of light showed in front of him. The voice he heard when he entered, said, "Are you ready for some light?"

Bill nodded, then felt silly. No one can see me in this darkness.

Before he could speak the host said, "Let there be light."

The pinprick grew to a glow, which grew brighter and brighter. At last, a subdued radiance bathed the room, and he could see the entire closet. It was larger than most of the ones in the house, but he estimated its size at nine by thirteen feet and it was a perfect rectangle. How the devil did I take seventeen steps and not find a corner?

"This room is deceptive," his host said. "I'm not surprised you seem confused."

Bill looked toward the sound of the voice. "How did you know what I was thinking?"

"I know much about you. Shall we continue our journey?"

"What journey? Where? I don't even know what to call you."

"Host would be fine."

Bill frowned. He didn't remember using that term aloud. So, he sees in the dark and reads minds. What else?

"That's about all," the host said. "If you don't like Host, I'm often called Watcher."

"Okay, Watcher. Tell me what I'm doing here and where would our journey take us?"

"Fair enough," Watcher said. "From time to time we—my brethren and others I represent—need to correct the direction of the universe. And by the way, it will be your journey. I will not actually accompany you." He paused as if to give Bill time to digest his words. "Occasionally, we identify an occurrence in the past that if left as is, will bring disharmony to the continuum. When that happens, I am called upon to contact someone like you to put the past right."

"I'm not liking the sound of this," Bill said. "It seems like time travel and I don't think I believe in that."

"You will believe. Before our journey is over, you will believe. Here, take this." Watcher extended an arm and gave Bill a small object. It had a luminescence of its own and looked like a cross between a cell phone, a television remote control and something from Star Trek. "If you lose this Union, you will not be able to communicate with me or return to the present. It is your lifeline to all that you know and without it, you might remain locked in the past. As long as you keep the Union with you, I can speak to you while you travel. I will call you Traveler."

"Can someone take it away from me and use it in my place?"

"No." Watcher explained the operation of the Union and said he would not only be able to communicate with Bill, but also visualize what he was doing in his new location during the journey. He held out another object toward Bill, which looked like a key featuring an ornate bow consisting of four circles linked and open in the center. "Guard this quatrefoil key well, without it the Union becomes useless. When the Union becomes weak, it will make a beeping sound. Insert this key and the unit will be re-energized."

Bill stood staring at Watcher and pondering his current predicament. One of his own making—again.

"Are you ready to go?" Watcher said. "We must get to our task without delay."

"I need to tell Sarah I'll be gone."

"For now, it's best she not know any of this."

Bill nodded and Watcher began. "I am afraid my comments about the Union were aimed at reassuring you and not quite true. I will take the Union back—you will not need it for your particular journey." He reached out a hand and Bill relinquished the device. Watcher continued, "On your way to the closing on this home, you complained of a headache and were prepared to stop at a small drugstore for aspirin. Do you remember?"

Bill nodded again. "I decided I could manage the headache and drove by the drugstore."

"A few minutes after you passed the store, a young meth addict entered. Brandishing a gun, he demanded cash and drugs. Something set the man off and he shot and killed the pharmacist, a store clerk and either two or three customers. The police could not determine what triggered the rampage, because they found the addict dead near the front door with a self-inflicted wound to his head."

Bill shrugged and, in a voice, thick with impatience said, "What's that got to do with me?"

"Bill, first you must know Sarah is expecting your child. She isn't aware of her pregnancy yet." Watcher paused, then said, "Bill, in a few days, Sarah will go into the room she is considering as a nursery. That entire side of the house has been weakened by dry rot. The creaky floor will give way under her feet, and she will plunge all the way down to the basement…she and your child will die."

"But…the house inspector…he said the building was sound."

"I fear the man was more interested in the fee than the structure."

Bill's eyes widened with excitement. "I'll just keep Sarah out of the room until I am able to have the floor supports repaired."

"That will not be possible. One thing I've neglected to mention to you…You have two ways to exit this closet—back through the closet door into your house…or through the opposite end, which is a portal to the past. In either case, once you leave this room, you will not remember the choices you make here. You cannot leave and use anything you learn here to protect your family in the present. You will however, have the opportunity to adjust the present by changing the past—but the choice must be made here…now."

Bill's shoulders slumped. "Do you mean I have a choice of living if I stop at that drugstore?"

Watcher's voice was low. "No. Remember I said 'either two or three' customers were killed there? If you stop, you will be the third customer to die that day…and Sarah will not complete the purchase of this house…and will be safe. I am sorry, but you do not have much time to make your decision."

Bill's head sagged and his chin touched his chest. How can I give up my wife or my child or…

He was quiet for several minutes. It took all his strength to raise his head and announce, "I've made my choice." There was a smile on his face as he moved forward toward the exit.

Watcher smiled too.

* * *

Sarah bent her head down so she could kiss the baby's forehead. She looked up at a nurse, in starched whites, marching into the hospital room.

The nurse held a clipboard. "Gotta have a name for the kid to go on the birth certificate. What is it?"

Sarah provided the nurse with the full name, spelling all three names.

"That's kinda a funny middle name" starched-whites said.

"Right after we were married, my husband told me it was an old family name."

The nurse wagged her head and shrugged her shoulders. "Ain't no skin off my nose." Then she turned and marched back out of the room.

Sarah gave the small child—William Watcher Ross—another kiss. Then she smiled.

The Watcher smiled too.

THE END